A Killing in Real Estate

K. K. Wolfe

ISBN-13: 978-0986247606 (Little Pencil Press)

ISBN-10: 098624760X

DEDICATION

This book is dedicated to Valerie Zehl, who harassed me endlessly until I wrote a book.

1 CHAPTER ONE

I was late for work, as usual. Jumping out of the car, grabbing my bag, purse and a plastic bag containing what passed for lunch these days, I ran for the front door. The parking lot was right in front of the building, so it was a short sprint. But as I rounded the big SUV that belonged to the office secretary, my flying foot caught on something and I went down in a heap, just short of cracking my skull on the brick wall beside the front door.

"What the hell is this?" I said. When startled, my level of civilization tends to slip just a touch, as was evinced by my language.

I pushed myself up while watching my lunch roll down the sidewalk toward the slushy edge of the parking lot. The orange that had been my lunch kept on going and I silently cursed the laws of physics that would take the damn thing and roll it right under my car so I would have to crawl through the dirty snow to retrieve what was a) all I could afford, and b) all my rather substantial body needed. I got up on one knee then stood up, still clutching the rest of my bags. I looked down to see what I had flown over. My stomach took an unaccustomed lurch as I saw a gray wool lump with an arm sticking out of it. I took one step toward it and moved around to the side to get a little better look, although I didn't really want a much better look. There, half turned down in the slush, was a face. A not-very-healthy looking one either, I might add. It appeared to be attached to the rest of the gray lump, which turned out to be an overcoat. Two legs and another arm stuck out of the overcoat. For all intents and purposes this thing had the proper parts to be a human.

Of course, along my sojourn through life I have run into creatures with two arms, two legs and a face that were not fit to be called human, but I am getting off the subject. By now, the realization was dawning that I was standing outside my office door staring at a person on the ground who had not reacted in the least to being walloped by one of my size 11 wides. How could that be? Easy. He was dead.

As soon as that thought started traveling through my sluggish little cranial vacuum, the part of my brain that is hooked to the panic button woke up. I yanked open the door and went tearing through the small lobby, down the hall, yelling "Fire," no, wait - wrong. "Dead guy. There's a dead guy outside." I never was good at screaming, so it came out in an almost-calm voice that belied my growing dread.

The only occupant of the room was our secretary, Bronislawa. At the sound of my barely excited voice, she turned slowly from the filing cabinet. Her large, pale blue eyes bore down on my face with their characteristic penetration. One of the guys in the office (who never failed to call her Brontosaurus), said those eyes could freeze a freshly baked pot-pie at 20 paces. The Birds-Eye people could use her. However, right now, I needed her to call the police or the undertaker or whoever is appropriate in this kind of a problem. I had never run across this before so I was a little new at deciding the next step. Besides being a little shaken up.

Bronislawa is about six foot one and does not divulge her weight. Not that anyone has dared ask, mind you. The rest of us have hazarded guesses between 240 and 280. I do not like to participate in this sort of thing because it seems a bit cruel and besides, I myself am not exactly petite. So I presume that if I don't try to guess someone else's weight, no one will bother with mine. This may or may not be true, but I prefer to believe it. It fits in with the rest of my fantasies.

So, in considering the present crisis, I hoped that she would live up to her image and be unflappably cool, calm and collected and without further ado, just dial up the police then continue filing.

Alas, this was not to be. Bronislawa's eyes kept getting bigger and bigger. I hoped they would stop soon because if they didn't, the stuff in her head behind her eyes would start to show around the edges and I really didn't want to see this. For all I knew there would be visible brain tissue any minute. Fortunately, they stopped, but then her mouth opened. It didn't say anything, but just flapped up and down and back and forth. Between the big eyes and the mouth that seemed to have a life of its own, I got the distinct impression I was gazing into an aquarium.

Finally the flapping slowed somewhat and noises began issuing from the still-gyrating hole in her face.

"Dead guy?" was all that came out, but it was a start.

"I think so. I tripped over him and he didn't move. We need to call somebody." I finally managed to get three semi-informative sentences arranged and verbalized.

Bronislawa lurched toward her desk, knocking the telephone off its cradle but rather neatly catching it mid-air with a large shaky hand. She punched in one number and then looked up at me.

"What is the number of the police?"

I wondered which number she had already hit and why, but decided not to make an issue of it.

"Just use 911," I said, very proud of myself that my brain was beginning to take over.

"Oh, good idea. I use that one. I saw it on the TV."

I realized that Bronislawa was starting to recover from shock a little because she was able to mention her beloved TV. She also hung up the phone, picked it up again and pecked out 911.

In the meantime I looked down the hall toward the front windows. I was too far away to see if our friend was still there. We were located in a little strip plaza along a fairly busy street, but no one else had come into the office yet. It must be that no one had gone into the office next door either. It was still early and there were very few people coming into the parking lot. The body (if that's what it was) was concealed from the street by Bronislawa's vehicle. She had an SUV that was appropriate for her size so it, too, was hard to see around.

We heard the sirens and went toward the front of the building. I didn't want to go out there until the police got here. I was a little surprised that Bronislawa had no curiosity about this. I guess looking like the Rock of Gibraltar and acting like it are two different things. She stood in the middle of the small lobby and didn't go near the front windows. We saw a police car pull up in front of the door and a lone village cop get out. He had a rather bored look on his face as he started toward the front door. His nearly falling over the body helped change that. He stopped short and appeared to be holding something back. I hoped it was his breakfast. With all due respect to the policeman, our little village doesn't have much crime. I doubted that this guy had ever seen a real dead body outside a funeral home before. I know I hadn't. When he looked up and saw us watching him, he tried to calm down some. He pulled his phone from his belt and called somebody. I assumed it was backup or whatever they call it on TV.

"He's calling for backup," Bronislawa spit out almost cheerfully.

That confirmed the TV connection. Bronislawa's family had come to this country from somewhere near the Baltic Sea when she was a teenager. Much to her credit, she spoke English with only a slight accent and some eccentricity in her sentence structure. Also she had a habit of using phrases she had picked up from the TV. After working with her for the last eight years, I can only assume her tastes run to television programs that dramatize unsolved mysteries involving crimes against prostitutes. Because we have members of the public coming into our office, we have had to censor some of Bronislawa's applications of American slang. I understand that when phrases are used repeatedly on television programs they can become burned into a person's subconscious and surface almost without effort. The problem arises when some of these are applied to a client's situation. It had appeared to her that the young ladies on the crime shows were dressed in what would pass for the latest fashions in some circles, wore lots of makeup and had glamorous hair styles. Taking all this into account, the word "slut" had translated into "attractive young lady," according to Bronislawa's interpretation of her adopted culture. So in Bronislawa's world, "book the slut" was synonymous with recording a client's contract in the sales records. She was positive that our clients would find it flattering. We had to carefully and with some sensitivity pry that particular phrase out of her everyday vocabulary. It took a while to convince her that less colorful is sometimes the way to go. I have to admit she is absolutely right that "reporting the sale" doesn't have the same ring to it as "book the slut."

But I am off on a tangent again.

The nice young policeman came into the lobby after he made his phone call.

"Did either of you see anything?" Dick Tracy asked.

I couldn't resist. "Yes, a body."

At that our crack sleuth dropped his notepad. He tried to bend down with a certain athletic grace to fetch it off the floor. The effect of the tight blue uniform pants was not lost on either Bronislawa or me. While we were trying to gauge the degree of muscularity through the cloth, he banged his head on the front desk as he came up. That pretty much blew the athletic grace aspect and we were both sidetracked by trying to keep a straight face as he once again faced us with his notepad open and no pen in hand. He quickly grabbed a pen out of his shirt pocket.

"A body?" he said.

"Yes, the one lying on the sidewalk. You can't miss it."

Ordinarily I am a bastion of mature behavior. Something about this morning's discovery was causing me to behave like a much younger, prettier version of Don Rickles.

The cop, who was about the age of my older son, looked up at me with the pity reserved for the slightly dotty elderly person and said, "How long has he been there?"

I bit my tongue before it could spit out "since last Tuesday" and tried to offer a chronology with the dignity befitting my age.

"I don't know. I just got here. I saw him when I got out of my car."

He turned toward Bronislawa, who was grinning like a large Baltic Cheshire cat, if there is such a thing. Her dream of being involved in a crime worthy of her favorite TV shows totally overshadowed the tragic nature of the event.

"Ma'am, did you see anything?"

"Ya, I see the dead man, just like she says."

"Did you also just get here?"

"No. I come in at seven o'clock to start the filing and the typing. There was no dead guy outside the door then."

The cop wrote all this down and looked up to see another police car pulling up to the front of the building.

"Excuse me, ladies."

He went outside to talk to the two plainclothes policemen who got out of the car. I was impressed. My knowledge of police departments is rather sketchy, not having Broni's level of experience with a TV, but I presumed that if they did not wear uniforms, then they were something important like detectives. I do have some knowledge of old movies and I don't remember Humphrey Bogart ever wearing a uniform. I didn't know that a small village department like ours would even have people like detectives. Or people like Humphrey Bogart either, for that matter.

At this point the three of them were looking at the body very carefully without touching it. The uniformed cop went to his car and returned with a roll of yellow tape that said "Crime Scene" all over it. He tied one end on the door handle and walked around Bronislawa's pride and joy, the Two-Ton Asphalt Masher. He hooked the tape around the back bumper and continued on down the parking lot a few feet, where he hooked it on a post sticking out of the ground and then back to the front of the building, where he tied the other end onto the door handle of the office next door. The tape created a rough rectangle surrounding the unfortunate gentleman on the ground.

Another police car pulled into the parking lot, which by this time was getting a little full. The lot is adequate for the building if you park correctly, but these guys were just zooming in and leaving their cars at angles across the middle, just like on TV, much to Bronislawa's delight.

Two uniformed guys got out of this car and sauntered over to the body. They conferred with the rest of the group, then the three uniforms started searching the parking lot, starting with the ground surrounding the dead guy.

I suppose this man has a name. He had just been the "dead guy" for going on 45 minutes now. I was beginning to wish they would do something with him instead of just letting him lie there. The initial shock of finding him was starting to wear off and I really felt bad that he was left on the ground in the cold. I had to remind myself that he probably wasn't bothered by the cold. My mental meanderings were interrupted by the plainclothes types coming in the front door. By now there was yet another vehicle in the parking lot. The van said "County Coroner's Office" on the side. There were two men kneeling on the ground looking at the body.

"May I have your name, please?" one of the men was asking.

Since he seemed to be looking at me, I said, "Yes, of course. Ophelia Olsen."

Ok, yes, it's my name. And yes, my nickname is "Oph." And yes, it's pronounced just like "Oaf." A great way to go through your childhood. Size 11 feet, five foot 10 and a beam the size of a small ocean-going dinghy. My mother was a fan of Shakespeare. I prefer not to delve into the reasoning behind naming me after a lunatic. Ophelia is also a moon of Uranus. Bad enough being named for a psychotic Dane.

"What do you do here?" he asked. I guessed correctly that this was still my question.

"I am a licensed real estate salesperson."

He looked up at Bronislawa. Up in a literal sense. She stood a good six inches taller than he did.

"Your name?"

"Bronislawa Zakresevskis."

His pen faltered a little on that one. I saw him write a 'Z,' a 'k', a 'v' and quit.

"Would you spell that, please?"

Bronislawa dutifully and very slowly spelled out all 12 letters. She knew from the TV that they needed the correct spelling and was proud to be of help.

"What do you do here?"

"I am the secretary. I type letters and file things and make the sales reports on the computer."

I cringed a little at that one. Bronislawa's acquaintance with the computer was shaky at best. I was glad the machine sitting on her desk didn't understand Livonian. I was glad I didn't either. Apparently from what I gather when I can understand the ramblings is that Bronislawa learned some choice phrases at the knee of an ancient great-grandmother who emigrated with the family from some part of Latvia. The Livonians were the original settlers of the coast of the Gulf of Riga way back. They had been gradually pushed aside and swallowed up by the subsequent Slavic settlers. In recent times they had been oppressed by the Russians until the USSR collapsed. By this time her family had come to this country to start over. Even in Latvia the Livonians constituted a very small percentage of the population. At one count there were only a few hundred people who could speak Livonian. Now that the great-grandmother has traded in her colorful folk garb for angel's wings, there is one less. So probably no one in our little town was going to understand what Broni was calling the computer. Even in Latvia the chances were slim. My concern was that she restrict her abuse of the office computers to the verbal kind. I am the geek in the office. It's my responsibility to make sure the computers work and perform any repairs that are necessary. I also occasionally sell a house.

The detective asked for both our addresses. We took turns giving him the information. The other plainclothes type sauntered over to the couch near the front window, opening up a little notepad and getting a pen out of his shirt pocket.

"Ms. Olsen, what time did you arrive this morning?"

"About 45 minutes ago." I looked at the clock to see what time it was now.

"Around 8:30 then," he said, writing.

"That would be about right." After looking at the clock I guessed it was about right.

"And how did you find the body?"

"I tripped over it," I said.

The detective looked up, "You tripped over it?"

"Yes, I was coming from my car." I pointed out the window at my little black car parked in the lot. "And as I came around the front of Bronislawa's car, I tripped over the body. It was in front of her car and I didn't see it," I explained, trying to dispel any possibility that I was a klutz.

"Miss, uh, Zakuhski, what time did you get here this morning?"

"Zakresevskis. I arrived upon the scene at seven a.m. I always get here at seven a.m. That is when I start the filing and the typing." Bronislawa enunciated and stood straight and tall and looked him right in the eye. Just like the witnesses on TV.

He looked at her. I think it was the reference to "arriving on the scene."

"Was the body here when you arrived?" he asked her.

"Oh, no. There was no body on the ground when I got here. If there was, I would have called the police right away," Broni answered with slight indignation.

I piped up and said, "The first policeman has already taken all this information."

The detective gave me a look that one would associate with either indigestion or smelling something bad.

"Do you have any objection to answering questions?" he said.

I realized Bronislawa was giving me a look, too. One that said I had just violated some important rule of police interrogation.

"Oh, no, of course not. I was just trying to save you some work." I smiled as graciously as is possible when one is not Miss America material. I noticed he did not smile back.

"Were you in any way acquainted with the body?"

"Only briefly, as I tripped over him. We hadn't met before that," I answered, trying to be helpful.

By now Bronislawa was looking at the floor. She was far more conversant with questioning protocol than I.

"I mean, no, I didn't know him. At least I think not. I didn't really see his face very well." As soon as I said that, I knew I had made a big mistake.

The detective looked up and said, "In that case, we're going to have both of you look at him before they take him away and see if you recognize him."

Bronislawa had a look of horror on her face mixed with the excitement of a once-in-a-lifetime chance of acting out her favorite gory crime show. I hoped this didn't presage our education in some kind of obscure Livonian rituals involving the deceased. The detective opened the door for us and we followed him out onto the sidewalk. Our visitor was still on the ground. The police people and the coroner's people were taking pictures and looking for any clues as to the cause of death.

"Can you turn him a little so these ladies can get a good look at his face?"

"Yeah, we're about done here. Detective, take a look at the big chunk of ice over there," said the man from the coroner's office as he rolled the victim's head to the side and pulled off his hat.

Bronislawa was crossing herself and muttering in what was probably Livonian.

"Do you know this man?" the detective asked.

"No, I don't. He doesn't look at all familiar," I said. After which I realized that he did look vaguely familiar. He looked like Bronislawa, but only in a kind of ethnic generality. He had a wide head, large bones, and a broad Slavic face and seemed to be rather tall, although it was hard to tell, what with him lying down.

I looked at Bronislawa. She was wobbling her head sideways this time, probably a negative.

The detective finished examining the piece of ice and opened the door to let us back in to the office.

I was glad to get away from the body. I didn't like thinking about how the poor man died.

The detective extracted a couple of business cards from his jacket pocket and handed one to each of us. The card said "Hubert Crowley" and indicated he was a detective. I must have smiled a little when I saw the Hubert, because he immediately spoke up.

"People call me Bert and if either of you see or hear anything that could be related to this gentleman or his death, call me immediately."

"Oh, yes, we will. Right away," I managed to babble.

Broni wobbled her head up and down.

The other detective came in from the parking lot. He nodded to the first one and said, "They're all done here. They'll have a report by tomorrow."

My eyes got big. "Does it look like murder?"

Bert Crowley nodded. "Possibly. He seems to have a very big lump on the top of his head. The large piece of ice could have done it. But there do not seem to be other icicles or chunks hanging from the building, so we will need to investigate. It is possible that someone used it to attack the gentleman. Ladies, that information is not for anyone else. Keep it to yourselves for now, please. How late are you open at night?"

"I'm not usually here in the evening, just once in a while. There may be other people here at night until eight or nine sometimes," I said.

In a shaky voice, Broni said, "I leave at four."

The second one said, "Tell any people that are here at night to watch for anything unusual and call us right away."

"Good-bye, ladies. Don't forget to call if you see or hear anything and until we know if this was accidental or deliberate, please be careful," said Hubert Crowley as he exited.

2 CHAPTER TWO

Broni went back to her filing and typing and I went into my office and sat down behind the desk. I just sat there for several minutes in a minor state of shock. I had never tripped over a dead body before. And to do it right in front of the very doorway that I entered nearly every morning. I stared at the wall for a few more minutes, aware of a growing sense of responsibility. This man fell down or was killed right in our doorway. Is there a cosmic code of retribution that made me this man's keeper? Do I need to avenge his death? No, this is not my problem. There is some insidious chemical additive in my instant oatmeal that is twisting my brain into thinking I can don a black jumpsuit and turn into Emma Peel. Emma Peel was the female half of the "Avengers," a 1960s British adventure series with spy/detective types John Steed and Emma Peel. They rode off in a sporty little English roadster, solved crimes involving very high-level international criminals by using John Steed's umbrella sword and Emma Peel's high kicks in pointy-toed boots and rode home again to drink champagne by the fireside, all in the space of 26 minutes. There are many reasons why this entire line of thinking is ludicrous. The first, and not least of the problems, would be to find a black Spandex jumpsuit in my size. I suspect perhaps Michelin would be the place to start. Secondly, Emma Peel subdued her enemies by running around doing what looked to me like karate or some such Oriental flailings, which usually ended up in her kicking these people in the head with the aforementioned pointy-toed boots, all the while remaining quite glamorous This required getting her foot a goodly distance off the ground. Depending on the size of the bad guy, this could be approximately three feet higher than my foot has ever gone.

Broni came to the door and stared at me.

"Are you feeling well? You look odd," she said.

I looked up at her, still with thoughts of running down Main Street in black Spandex catching important international criminals occupying the upper portion of my cranial tissue.

"How do you mean that?" I said, indignant that anyone would have such disrespect for a superstar crime-fighting Spandex-clad beauty such as myself.

"Just like I said. You look odd in the face."

"I was just thinking. That dead guy was somebody. He had a name and probably a family of some kind and maybe a job. How did he get here? If he was murdered, who killed him? Why did they kill him? It's very curious. Don't you wonder about this?" I wondered if Broni had noticed the man's vague ethnic resemblance to her.

Broni's face took on a kind a sympathetic aspect, like when you look at a relative who isn't quite right in the head as she said, "No. It isn't good to know too much about these things. Sometimes it can be dangerous."

"How can it be dangerous? He isn't connected to us. Who would want to harm us? He just happened to land outside our door."

Broni's face sank from the previous pitying state to one of slight horror. "No, you can't know some things."

She looked around to make sure no one was listening, even though we were the only two people in the office. I sensed an ancient Livonian proverb was about to be uttered.

"The reindeer knows not what lies beyond the tip of the antler." She muttered in a low gravelly voice that I suspected was the same tone used to relate this ancient piece of wisdom to her.

"Let me guess. Your grandmother?"

Broni slowly shook her large head up and down. "My grandmother was one of the wise ones of the village. She had the sight in the forehead."

I assumed that she meant her grandmother had some kind of ESP or clairvoyance rather than an actual third eyeball. Yet, on the other hand, after hearing her describe some of her second cousins, I wondered.

On a few other occasions, when the severity of the situation called for it, Broni had shared with us some of her grandmother's other wisdoms. A lot of them seemed to revolve around farm animals, a group that apparently shared a level of intelligence with some of those second cousins, which may be an insult to some of the farm animals.

"Oph, did you not notice that the deceased looked like a Northern European type? If this is true, he may have some connection to us, or to me, at least."

"So you did notice. He looked like he could be related to you. Do you have any relatives floating around in this country?"

"Only some cousins that may be in this country, or they may be in jail somewhere unknown. Oph, this could be frightening. I don't think we should be involved."

"We're not really involved, I was just curious about the poor man, that's all. Don't be scared, I'm not really going to change into black Spandex."

I should not have said that. Broni looked at me with a far deeper sense of pity than before.

"Never mind. Did you want something?"

"I need you to come look at my computer. It doesn't work so good."

She waved at me to follow her. I reluctantly gave up my Emma Peel fantasy and got up out of my chair with what I thought was a lithe and supple movement, crashing my left hip into the corner of my desk, causing me to emit a yelp that sounded nothing like a world-famous spy. Broni just looked and shook her St. Bernard head back and forth while rolling her giant blue reindeer eyes. Reindeer are one of the few animals that can change their eye color depending on the season. Scientists have observed that reindeer have blue eyes in the winter. Broni is a perpetual winter reindeer.

I worked on the computer just long enough to find out there wasn't really anything wrong with it. Mostly operator error or, in computer terms, a nut loose behind the mouse.

By now the crime scene tape was cleared from the front of the building and people were starting to pull into the parking lot. The small crowd that had gathered out on the street, gawking at the police cars and coroner's van, had dissipated as soon as the official vehicles had pulled out. A few straggled to the laundromat next door and the coffee shop a few doors down. Larry Smith came through the door. He is a real estate agent in our office and was scheduled to be answering the telephone this morning. It was a few minutes after 10. He was supposed to be here at nine.

"Floor time start at 10 now, Larry?"

He looked at me like I just got off a ship from Mars.

"I wasn't coming in here with all those cop cars out there. They had the front door blocked off. What happened?"

Oh, how quickly we forget. "Oh, you're right, there was body in front of the door this morning."

Larry's eyes bugged out. "A body? What kind of body?"

"A dead one."

Larry looked like he was going to faint dead away. His mouth was flapping open in a fish-like motion akin to Bronislawa's earlier display.

"Relax. It's gone now," I said in a comforting manner.

He sat down at the front reception desk. His mouth was still flapping. He pulled a grayed, slightly tattered handkerchief out of his pocket and wiped his forehead. I could sympathize with him. I felt like the office would never be the same safe, unassuming place it once was. Larry was not a brave kind of guy. He was rather quiet and lived a quiet life. This would be a major shake-up in his secure routine.

I have to admit that this was a blow to my safe, secure daily routine also. Finding death on your doorstep in the morning is not the way I want to wake up. I was trying to be very cool about this for Larry's sake, but I was afraid my armor had a few little chinks in it. Like the pen shaking as I wrote in the Daily Log on the front desk, hoping Larry wasn't paying attention. I wondered if I should put the dead guy in the log book and decided against it, not knowing how to make a tasteful entry under the circumstances.

I walked back up to the front of the office and looked out the window. My eyes kept going to the spot on the sidewalk where the body had been. There hadn't been any blood on the sidewalk. What did the policeman say? He may have been killed by falling ice? It must be that didn't necessarily leave any blood. The guy had a hat on. One of those mad bomber hats with the ear flaps like they wear in really cold places.

It turned out to be a bright, beautiful day. I looked up when I saw a shadow cross the sidewalk and sunshine reflecting off a partially bald head surrounded by a crown of white hair. Someone was waving at me. It was Mr. Bosch. He stopped in the office almost every day to have a cup of coffee. He owned a vacuum cleaner store a couple of blocks down the street.

"Hello. How are you?" he said as he came through the door.

I guess I didn't answer right away.

"What's wrong, Oph?" he said as he leaned up against the reception counter. "You look odd."

"That's the second time somebody has told me that this morning," I said.

Larry was looking up from behind the desk below the counter.

"You both look odd; what's going on?" Mr. Bosch remarked.

"Well, it's like this. When I came into the office this morning, I tripped over a dead body."

Mr. Bosch then got an odd look on his face too. "A dead body?"

I shook my head up and down.

"Who was it?"

"We don't know. The police came and blocked off the parking lot for a while. They asked some questions and then took the body away," I explained.

"That's what all the commotion was. When I drove past here this morning I saw some police cars, but I couldn't see what was going on. There were too many people out on the sidewalk. I thought maybe the laundromat got broken into or something. Boy, I always thought this was a quiet place. I've had my vacuum cleaner shop in the same spot for 32 years and never heard of anything like this."

"We're all feeling a little spooked by this, I think. I can't get the picture of it out of my head," I volunteered.

Larry was still sitting there a little ashen-faced, shaking his head, which caused his wispy dishwater blond strands to flop in a most unattractive manner. " I've lived here all my life. It's hard to think about it happening right here. Why did it happen here?"

I was a little annoyed with Larry. He was concerned with his world being changed, but not with who this guy was or the fact that this had affected all of us, most notably the dead guy.

Mr. Bosch turned to look out the front window. "What did this man look like? Is he anybody you recognized?"

"No. I don't remember ever seeing him before. He looked a

little bit familiar, but then I realized it was because he looks like Broni. Kind of a wide head and blond hair. Probably a tall guy and rather big-boned. He had on an overcoat of some kind. Sort of brownish grey or tweedy." I finished describing the body and looked at Mr. Bosch. He was staring at me with wide eyes and gray skin, while nervously picking at his left ear.

"Are you alright? Now you're the one that looks odd," I said as I put my hand out toward him.

Mr. Bosch said, "Oh, I'm fine, I have to go now. It's time to open the shop."

"Don't you have time for your cup of coffee?" I asked him as he was turning toward the door.

"No, no, not today." Mr. Bosch made a hurried exit and we watched him walking very fast in the direction of his vacuum cleaner store.

3 CHAPTER THREE

"That was strange," said Larry, looking out the window at the back of Mr. Bosch's raincoat as it disappeared down the street.

I also thought Mr. Bosch's reaction was strange. One of the few times I have agreed with Larry. I walked into my office and picked up a sheaf of papers. I had to go on a listing appointment in half an hour and needed to clear my mind of the events of the morning so I could settle down to business. I looked over the market analysis I had done on the prospective property to make sure it was as accurate as possible. I gathered my business cards, the listing contract and grabbed my purse and car keys, yelled back to Broni that I would be gone for an hour or so and told Larry the same thing. I got in my car for the short drive to the house. I was trying to keep my mind on the task at hand, but the slippery little brain cells kept wandering back to the dead guy. There was now a new wrinkle: Mr. Bosch's reaction.

I pulled up to the house and sat in the car for a couple minutes to clear my head again. I hoped I wasn't going to have to do this too much. Clearing my head is a lot of work. It always seems to have all sorts of unusual things running around in there.

I managed to make it through the listing appointment, get the contract signed, put up the yard sign and get back to the office in an hour and a half. I parked my car in the end spot again, which had miraculously remained empty while I was gone. I got out of the car and took the same path around Broni's Lumberjackmobile that I had taken this morning. It hit me all of a sudden as I approached the door. I stopped and looked down at the sidewalk again, imagining a body lying there. The sun had come out and I could see a small round glint of sunlight up against the brick front of the building beside the door. I kneeled down to get a closer look, trying to not to get a creepy feeling about kneeling in this spot. It looked like a small silver-colored disk, like a coin. I started to pick it up and stopped. What if this belonged to our body? I should know better. I can hear Broni now. "Don't touch evidence." I was fresh out of rubber gloves, so I went in the door and yelled for Broni.

"Bring me one of those sandwich bags under the kitchen sink. I need an evidence bag."

That may have been cruel. I knew once she heard "evidence bag" she would drop whatever she was doing and come running. Sure enough, in three seconds flat she was at the door with a clean sandwich bag.

"What did you find? Where is it?" She was still gasping for breath.

"Out here," I went back out the door. "See, down here, a little coin." I turned the bag inside out and stuck my hand inside the bag to pick up the coin without touching it. I then pulled the bottom of the bag back through and zipped it shut.

"There. Now we give it to the police." I started toward the phone.

Broni was staring at the bag." Let me see, please."

"Ok, but leave it in the bag," I said.

She looked at me like pond scum. The queen of prime-time police shows was insulted.

"Yeah, ok, here, have a look," I said, scuttling off to the

phone. By the time I was finished talking to the desk sergeant (Broni told me what he was), she was done examining the coin.

"This is a bracteat," she proudly announced.

"A what?" I said.

"A bracteat," she repeated more slowly this time, so my feeble brain could catch it.

"Ok, I give up. What is a bracteat?"

"A bracteat is like your penny. Only it is from the Livonian civilization in the Middle Ages. They were made in probably the 1300s or 1400s. They were also called dunnpfennig. They eventually were not used because they were tiny and too much work to count."

"So, is this bracteat worth a lot of money?" I asked our walking encyclopedia of Livonian culture.

"No. Not so much. Maybe 50 or 70 dollars."

"The second question is: Why would it be out in front of our building? If this fell out of the dead guy's pocket, does that mean he is a Livonian?"

Broni looked at me again with the pity reserved for the slightly feeble of mind. "Remember, according to the 2000 Latvian census there were 177 Livonians. The surrounding Baltic cultures took over the Livonians. Also the Swedes once ruled, so there is a big mixture of all kinds of people. Sort of like here in the U.S."

"But aren't you sort of Livonian?" I asked, trying to salvage my intellectual credibility and not betray my ignorance of the 2000 Latvian census.

"Yes, but only by my grandmother, whose family lived in an isolated little village. Even then she had some other cultures, too, she just didn't like to say so. She used as much of the Livonian dialect as she knew to hand it down to her children and grandchildren."

I was trying to assimilate this crash course in Livonian

culture. "So if this guy was Livonian, he is one of only 177 of them?"

"Yes. Now you have it." Broni beamed at having taught me something.

So now I have it, but what am I going to do with it?

"Broni, I told the policeman on the phone I would take this coin to them. I guess I had better tell them you identified it, too, although there is a coin dealer just a couple of blocks from them. They can get it looked at if they want. I think I will go home after that. I'll see you tomorrow. I'll have the paperwork on that new listing done, too."

"You had better. It has to be in the system by tomorrow."

The desk sergeant at the station took my little bag and looked it over. He took my name and I told him about the coin. He looked at me rather quizzically.

"How do you know so much about this coin?"

"The secretary in my office knows all about the Livonians. Her grandmother was a Livonian and taught her about the culture and language. There are only 177 of them left in the world," I proudly recited and hoped I had remembered it correctly.

"Where did you find this, again?" the sergeant asked.

"Right outside the front door to the office. Very close to where the body was found this morning," I repeated.

"So you think this belonged to the deceased?"

"I think it is a reasonable possibility, considering its location and the fact that no one ever noticed it before and if it had been there, our eagle-eyed Livonian secretary probably would have spotted it." I was getting just a mite annoyed with this police person.

"Ok, Ms. Olsen, I will give it to Detective Crowley. He is working on the case."

"Thank you and I'm sure the deceased would thank you, too," I added as I turned to go out the door.

4 CHAPTER FOUR

I pointed my car toward home. I lived only about two miles
north of the police station in a big old Victorian house just
outside the village. It was close enough to the office to walk,
but if I had an appointment to show a house or get a listing I
needed my car with me. Consequently, I didn't walk much. As I
got to the last corner before my house, I decided to pull into the
grocery store and pick up cat food. It appears that much of the
money I spend on groceries is used for something other than
people food. I shared my house with George and Ira. They
were brothers, just as the original George and Ira were, but this
George and Ira were somewhat shorter (although not a lot from
what I understand) and covered with gray fur. Ira has a white
patch on his face, whereas George has more gray. They both
have white socks. Furwise, of course. Neither plays the piano.

I pulled into my driveway and punched the box on my visor.
The garage door opened and I wondered if Emma Peel had a
garage door opener like this. She probably did, but her garage
and the door would be camouflaged to look like a small hill or a
large clump of bushes or a small hill covered with bushes.
When she hit the button, a portion of hill/bushes would rise,
allowing her entrance into the secret cave. As I drove into my
cave/garage I was looking up trying to judge how much space
was between the door and the edge of the door casing. It didn't

look like enough to be able to paste some bushes on the front of the door. My musings were interrupted by my car slowly rolling into the wood pile in front of me. I stopped rather abruptly and hoped no international criminals were lurking outside, watching my ignominious entrance. I got my stuff out of the car, punching the button to close the garage door, and went up the sidewalk toward the house. As I unlocked the back door, I could hear the characteristic thumpings of my welcoming committee. I opened the kitchen door and found four eyes staring at me. George and Ira were lined up on the floor. They have the idea that if they greet me at the door with such fanfare, that I will be fooled into thinking it is dinner time.

"Hello, guys. It's only 3:30. Not dinner time yet." That was met by a chorus of trills and chirps protesting my interpretation of time. By their standards, dinnertime was any time after the breakfast food was gone.

I set down my bags and walked through the dining room into the den. I looked at the answering machine. No messages, but that was nothing new. Today even the telemarketers had ignored me. The mail contained the usual missives from the gas company and the telephone company and whatever other vultures circled my mail slot on a regular basis. These I would take care of later when I had nothing better to do.

The first order of business was to change my clothes and decide if it was warm enough to work outside for a while before supper. I went up the stairs to my bedroom, with George and Ira trailing behind me. They weren't about to give up if they thought there was any chance they could trick me into thinking it was time to feed them. They sat on the bed on their respective blankets while I put on a pair of jeans, sneakers and an old sweatshirt. When working outside, I usually forsake the glamour. I tend to embrace the mud.

The three of us traipsed down the stairs with me telling them that I was going outside for a little while until it was time to eat and perhaps they could find a sun puddle to lie in or some dust bunnies to contemplate. I was treated to mournful looks as I went out the kitchen door.

The sun was bright, but the temperature hadn't caught up to it. The wind was brisk and I decided I would think of it as bracing. I'm not sure what bracing is, but when people in novels wanted to walk along the cliffs high above the sea, the wind was bracing instead of just "let's watch our knuckles turn purple in this damn cold wind." I got a rake out of the garage and tried to prioritize the sections of lawn as to urgency. It all looked like it needed work. There were little branches and twigs everywhere from the winter wind storms. Little piles of slushy, melting snow dotted the yard. I started in the lawn directly behind the house. It didn't really matter which one got done first. Raking is a nice mindless activity. It is also relatively quiet. It allows the mind to flow endlessly from one subject to another like a little babbling brook running through the woods, unless the babbling little mind gets stuck on one subject like mine just did. The man in the tweedy grayish brown overcoat with the bomber hat. Who was he? Did someone bang him over the head? They seemed to think the icicle could have done it. Couldn't the icicle have been used as a weapon by someone? They weren't looking for a sharp object. They mentioned something blunt because of the lack of visible damage. That doesn't make sense. The guy is dead. How much more damage can you do? The good thing about all this curiosity is that the time flew by, a good-sized part of one lawn was raked and it was time to go in and feed the furry ones. I put the rake back in the garage. They were waiting patiently at the kitchen door as I opened it while standing on the three steps up from the back door.

"Ok, guys. It is now supper time. What would you like tonight? The choices are liver and bacon, turkey and giblets or ocean whitefish."

The whitefish got the loudest reaction. Mostly from Ira. George didn't talk. He just circled my ankles, swatting at my sneaker laces. I split the can between the two bowls then went to the refrigerator to see what my choices were. I didn't have three. I had one choice. I think when there is only one, it isn't called a choice. I dragged the soup kettle out and set it on the big front burner and turned on the stove. I got a box of crackers out of the cupboard to add a little excitement to the soup. My secret soup recipe is little pieces of chicken and a couple of bags of frozen vegetables. The final touch is to put a ring of crackers around the inside of the bowl and a three-inch diameter pool of ketchup on top of the soup, just touching the edges of the crackers.

I savored my gourmet fare as I watched the six o'clock news. I wanted to see if there was any mention of our mysterious deceased person. I also remembered there hadn't been any television cameras or reporters swarming the parking lot today to get an interview from me. I guess they only go after the photogenic eyewitnesses. At the very end of the newscast, there was a mention of an as-yet-unidentified body being found in a parking lot in the village. There was a short video showing the front of our building and the parking lot, obviously taken from the street. I looked to see if either Broni or I were visible in the front window, but it looked empty. Oh, well. Broni will be disappointed. I'm sure her police dramas always have interviews with any possible witnesses on TV. Our problem is that the village of East Gilmore is on the outskirts of Buffalo, NY. We are a small place about 35 miles southeast, so our crimes don't get much attention. They have much bigger fish to fry much closer to home. The last time we were mentioned was obviously a slow news night. It involved a bored-looking, rookie reporter who did three minutes of video on Mrs. Slowinski's prize-winning cantaloupes.

After an uneventful evening of reading and conversing with

Ira, I went to bed. I read for a while then turned out the light. As I started to doze off, I wondered how to get the bushes to stick to the garage door.

5 CHAPTER FIVE

The morning dawned bright and too early. I awoke to the sight of four big golden eyeballs staring at me.

"Ok, I know it's time for breakfast. Just let me wake up for a few minutes."

I clicked the remote control and turned on the morning news. Same stuff: war, pestilence, famine and plagues and still nothing much about the man at the doorstep. Suzie Cute, or whomever the anchor was this week, read a short item about the still-unidentified man found deceased yesterday in a village parking lot. I guess they don't have much to say yet.

I crawled out of bed rather sluggishly, berating myself for not turning out the light earlier. I do this every morning. I staggered out of my bedroom across the library and into my bathroom with Ira right behind me. He stood on the counter watching me as I went through my morning ablutions. My beauty ritual came next. That's the name I've given it, even though the results don't justify the title. All the women I see on TV have beauty rituals, so I presume I need one, too. I can be certain Emma Peel had a beauty ritual. That was reason enough for me.

I headed to my closet to pick out my outfit. That was another phrase I had adopted from Those Who Were More Glamorous Than I. I noticed on TV, that "those people" didn't just get dressed, they "picked out outfits." My picking consisted of opening the closet door and moving a couple of hangers, grabbing whatever fell off first. With Ira right on my heels and George leading the way, we descended the stairs. In the kitchen, the can of salmon paté was opened and split between the two dishes. The sun was streaming in the kitchen windows. The bright blue sky was beautiful. I looked at the clock and determined that I had enough time for a bowl of bran flakes, which smelled much better than the salmon paté the boys were devouring. With the dishes in the dishwasher, the salmon and bran flakes consumed and my lunch orange in my red bag, I bid George and Ira adieu and departed. I opened the garage door, very disappointed that it still looked like a garage and not at all like a disguised spy hideout. The big disappointment came when I got into my little black Nissan that bore absolutely no resemblance to Emma Peel's baby blue Lotus Elan. I couldn't even get the top to go down. At least not without power tools.

I putted down the street toward the office. It was only a four-minute drive, so I could listen to one song on the CD player. I punched the button and out came a Barbra Streisand version of "I'm in the Mood for Love." Not exactly a morning song. Besides, I felt it necessary to sing along with every song, and this one had some high notes that were a real strain first thing in the morning. If the truth were known, they were a real strain at any time of day. I did my best to follow along and was working my way up the scale nicely when I had to stop at the red light a few blocks from home. That allowed me to concentrate on hitting the note and also build up some real volume. As I was moving my head around in appropriately theatrical gestures, I caught a glimpse of the guy sitting in the car next to me. He seemed to be amused by something. He must have been listening to a funny thing on the radio. I don't know why he was staring at me. Maybe my beauty routine had finally taken.

The rest of the four-minute trip was uneventful and I pulled up to the office to park the car. As I saw Broni's two-ton Power Polluter sitting there, I had a flashback of yesterday's events. We had a dead guy lying here. A person who still didn't have a name. When I was away from the scene, it didn't seem so real, but now I had a heavy feeling in my stomach again just like yesterday. The police said it might be murder. That means that whoever did this is still walking around. Possibly right here in the plaza. Was I really concerned over the poor dead guy or more concerned for my own skin? That is kind of embarrassing and makes me realize what a rotten person I can be. I should have been upset about this man losing his life. I was, to a certain extent, just before the self-preservation aspect took over. I gathered my purse and red bag and got out of the car. I started walking, then stopped abruptly. I turned around and went around the front of my car, down the other side, turned right onto the sidewalk, went forward toward the door. It didn't work. I still had to step on the place where the dead guy had lain. Since I was now right in front of the door, I opened it and went in. Enough is enough. He doesn't care if I step there, so why should I?

Feeling a little foolish, which is not a new situation for me, I walked through the door of my office. Setting my bags down, I sensed a larger-than-life presence behind me in the doorway. I turned around to face Broni, who was standing there with a blank, yet concerned look on her face. Not too many people can pull that off successfully. With most people, blank is blank. Adding character to blank takes a strong constitution.

"What's wrong?" I asked, somewhat fearful of the answer.

"I am being confused and puzzled," Broni said, dropping her eyes.

I took my time formulating the next question because when Broni says she is confused and puzzled, it could mean anything from having to skip over part of Einstein's theories to having forgotten where the ladies' room is.

I jumped in with, "About what?"

"The dead guy."

"Oh, Broni. I feel bad too, but we didn't even know him and I just wish the police could find out who he is and why he died. Especially why he died on our doorstep."

"No, no. My puzzlement comes from the bracteat."

I had to think fast on this one. Why was she referring to what sounded like a moss-covered bovine body part? Then it hit me, the coin! She was talking about the Livonian coin.

"Oh, that is puzzling. Why would a man here in the village be carrying a coin from Livonia? How old did you say it was?"

"I don't know. The age of a bracteat is hard to determine because they were made for many years. It is probably about 500 years old."

"Do Livonian people carry old coins, as a rule?" I said, fishing for Livonian customs.

"Not that I am aware. Maybe some people carry them for good luck." Broni looked unsure at that.

"Well, if anybody else is carrying one for good luck, I think we'd better tell them it doesn't work."

"Sure is damn tootin' right," Broni said. Occasionally her TV vocabulary strayed to old Westerns.

I sat down at my desk as Broni wandered off to the back of the office where her desk and beloved filing cabinets were. She had aroused my curiosity again. Why was that coin by the body? Livonians are rare. It's almost impossible that there would be two of them in one little village in America. Is that even significant? What was significant is that the guy had gotten himself into something unsavory or made one enemy too many. Had he done that here or before he got here?

I could feel my mind doing its identity shift thing again. My brain saw me clad in black Spandex with a baby blue Lotus parked out in front. John Steed would be calling any moment now to say "We're needed." We would rush off to find out who the dead guy was and why he was killed and twenty-six minutes later we would come back to drink champagne.

There are only two problems I can see with this scenario. My clothes have not changed since I left home. The old baggy blue skirt, old baggy top and old baggy sweater with the stretched-out shiny elbows did not very closely resemble Emma Peel's black Spandex and pointy-toed boots. Secondly, John Steed had not called and was not likely to, since he had never called. One more problem: the baby blue Lotus Elan. Do the clothes and the car really make the detective? Perhaps I would be more effective and less conspicuous without the flashy clothes and car. The problem is that the clothes and the car were all I cared about. I didn't really want to solve crimes.

Broni appeared at my door again. "What if he was Livonian? There are so few left, we need to find out so we can honor his life." She stood tall at the end of this pronouncement, the very image of a proud Livonian. At least I guess that's what a proud Livonian would look like.

"Broni, the police said he could have been murdered. Maybe his life didn't have much in it to honor, unless he ran afoul of some criminals. We don't know if he was the bad guy or his murderer is, or both." I held my breath for a moment, hoping I hadn't stirred up any Livonian pride.

To my relief, she said, "You are right." And then she said, "We need to find out who is the bad guy. We will track down the killer."

My eyebrows elevated themselves about two inches. "We? As in you and me? We are going to track down the killer? Yesterday you told me the reindeer shouldn't look beyond his antlers. Now you want to venture into unknown territory?"

Broni's large, square face looked as if it had been set in stone. She shook her head slowly up and down signifying that yes, she did mean that we would be out looking for a dangerous person.

"I have never tracked down a killer. I have a hard time finding flies that get in my house in the summer. I can't even find my car keys a lot of the time. When was the last time you did this? Do you know anything about finding a murderer?" At that, I thought I had better quit, since I knew very little about Broni's past. For all I knew she belonged to the Livonian version of the CIA. She looked insulted.

"It is just a matter of hard work. The detectives all say that if you keep looking, you will find the killer." At this she tilted her chin up and pointed out the front window in a TV-inspired dramatic moment, although she looked more like a golden retriever on the trail of a duck.

"Broni, I would really like to help you, but I am not very brave. I wouldn't know what to do if I found a killer. This could be dangerous. We could get hurt ... or worse."

I was starting to get a little scared because Broni looked so serious about this. She loosened up on her retriever pose and turned her head to face me.

"Will you not help me?" The blue-eyed stare.

I hung my head in shame. What would Emma Peel think of me? John Steed would never call with an attitude like this. Also, I had enough decency to know I couldn't let Broni do this on her own. It is time to try reason.

"We need to let the police do their job and find the killer. We might just be in the way and make things worse. We don't have guns or handcuffs or anything like that," I said as I looked at Broni, who gave me a look of pity.

"You don't have those things, do you?" I said as her face cracked into a slowly spreading smile. She probably had some hidden under her couch.

"Look, if it will make you feel better, let's go over to the police station and see if we can find that detective that was here yesterday and ask him if they know who the dead guy is. Maybe they have the case all wrapped up by now and the murderer is already in jail."

"All right. We will go and ask the police if this is true," Broni said rather impatiently.

"Good. We can go just as soon as the next duty agent comes in at noon. That's only a half hour."

Maybe something will happen in the next half hour to get me off the hook. Like an absolute miracle.

Don, the office manager, walked in and peeked in my office.

"What's going on this morning? Not as much excitement as yesterday, I hope."

"Hi. No, nothing like yesterday. So far today is pretty calm."

"Good. Got any sales or listings coming in anytime soon?"

I racked my brain to think up something to tell him. "I've got a listing to put in the system today or tomorrow."

"Glad to hear that. We need listings. There isn't that much on the market right now. The inventory's dropping. I hope this one isn't overpriced."

"No, this one is just perfect. A nice Cape Cod with only a little water in the basement. The kitchen was remodeled as recently as 1973 and the plywood in the broken windows has been painted to match the trim. If the new owners place their furniture just right nobody will ever see the burn marks in the carpet."

"Ok, sounds great." Don went off to his office. He wasn't the brightest bulb in the chandelier. It would dawn upon him sometime later today that I may have been pulling his chain. At that point I could tell him I was just kidding. To tell him now would be cruel. He has to process the information at his own speed. It's a lot like feeding corn to a goose. You just have to wait for the result. And try not to step in it.

Now I have to think of something to get Broni's mind off this Livonian corpse. If I get the paperwork all done on this listing, it will have to go in to the computer and that will keep her busy for an hour or so, long enough for me to leave, then come back and tell her the police are working on the case diligently and rejected our help.

I was furiously filling out the computer profile sheet containing the information on the property when my office went dark. It has no windows, so the only light comes through the door. That source of illumination was being blocked by our Bronislawa, with her hat on. Broni's mother made this hat. It was a traditional Latvian folk hat, which means it is shaped like a small cylindrical wastebasket, knitted in shades of brown and dark green with a red circle on the flat crown.

"Ready to go?" Broni said, with her big friendly grin.

"I have to have this listing finished so it can go into the system today. Maybe we should go later," I sniveled, trying to get out of this.

"The noon duty agent is here, and I am caught up in my typing and filing. I will enter your listing when we return. It will not take very long. Our mission is very important."

I looked up at her. I don't believe I have ever heard that many sentences at once out of her mouth. "Our mission"? Now I am getting scared. I reluctantly got to my feet and faced the door.

"Now, Broni, we can go to the police station and ask them some questions. You have to realize they may not want to answer them. I don't think they are particularly fond of people butting their noses into an investigation. I will go with you, but we are just going to ask how they are doing and then we will leave. Ok?"

Broni's blue eyes took on a different color. I swear they changed to a steel gray-blue. I retreated a step, wishing I had paid more attention to geography. Was Latvia anywhere near Transylvania?

"Ok. We will go and ask the questions. If they do not like us there we will leave. Come, I will drive."

I had just lost two battles without even knowing I was fighting them. First of all, I was going to the police station against my better judgment. Also against my better judgment I was riding with Broni in her 4000-pound Pavement Packer. Broni's driving habits are something she learned on TV, also. Unfortunately, not on shows that emphasized the rollover dangers of a vehicle with a high center of gravity. Her cornering technique was gleaned in bits and pieces from many car chases on her beloved crime programs. As we took off from the parking lot, I held on to the door handle for dear life. Broni gave me a sidelong glance that bespoke volumes about her opinion of me.

"You don't have to hang on so tightly. I have calculated the angle beyond which I cannot turn the car without the two outboard wheels leaving the surface of the road. We are only going three blocks and we will be there in three minutes with four turns." She recited all this while swishing the big truck in and out of traffic and around corners.

In her native country, Broni had gone to a science and mathematical high school. She had graduated at the age of 16, just before her family came here. It is not unusual to hear her spit out an answer based on combining a physical law with a mathematical calculation of some sort. In our office the most advanced calculation is liable to be figuring out the right amount of water to put in the coffee pot, but if we need any advanced stuff, we know where to turn.

Much to my amazement, we arrived at the station in one piece in exactly three minutes. I got down out of the truck, landing on the pavement with a slight exclamation. Broni came around the vehicle and we went up the brick steps. Inside the front door was the same desk sergeant that I talked to yesterday when I brought the coin to the station.

"Hello," I said in a cheerful voice designed to charm the policeman and win him over to our side.

"Can I help you ladies?" he replied, not yet reacting to my charm.

"Yes. We are inquiring about the body that was found yesterday in front of our office. We were wondering if he has been identified yet," I said in yet another attempt to smoothly ingratiate myself and my companion into his good graces.

"What is your interest in the case?" he responded.

I looked at Broni. She was calm, yet I could see her eyeballs beginning to get steely. I watched as her mouth began to move.

"We need to see Detective Crowley," Broni dictated to the young man.

I was surprised she knew the name, but then I saw that she had a business card in her hand. The detective had given them to us yesterday. I had already lost mine.

"Do you have any information about the deceased or the circumstances of his death?" the desk sergeant asked her.

"We need to see Detective Crowley," she repeated. Her eyes were moving, looking up and down the hallway in back of the desk. Suddenly her eyes stopped. I looked up to see what was so riveting. It was a sign sticking out from the wall in the hallway that said "Detective Hubert Crowley." Broni moved slowly around the desk, and down the hallway.

The sergeant started to stand up. "You can't go in there."

Broni kept moving slowly forward, pausing only to turn her head toward the sergeant. As she did I could see that she had that look in her eyes that could freeze a bag of peas at twenty paces. The sergeant looked as though he had been hit by an icicle. She kept on moving forward toward Detective Crowley's door. I was standing there like a goofy statue, afraid to move until I found out if the desk sergeant was going to be ok. He still looked a little stunned, but was coming out of it. I figured I had better get going before he recovered fully. I looked back at him, smiled and called out, "They're old friends."

Meantime Broni had her hand on the doorknob of the door under the Detective Crowley sign. She turned it and went in. I got to the door just in time to see Broni advancing on a desk, behind which was sitting a surprised gentleman. It was Detective Crowley.

"Good afternoon, Detective," Broni said in her best TV voice. "I have come to help you in your investigation of the dead person we found yesterday."

Much to his credit, Detective Crowley did not throw us out of the office immediately. In fact, he was quite a gentleman. I was impressed.

"Sit down, ladies," he said pointing at two straight-backed wooden chairs in front of his desk. "You've come to help?" The detective had the hint of a smile on his face as he said this. "This is about the body that your friend here found in front of your office. Is that right?"

"Yes. We will help you with the causes and motives for the murder," Broni said with her head held high, kind of like the Statue of Liberty, except with steely blue eyes and no torch.

Crowley leaned back in his chair and played with his pen cap. "How is that?"

"We think we know something about the victim."

I piped up with "Broni may know where he's from."

At that the detective looked a little more interested. He picked up a notebook off his desk and started flipping through it.

"It was Ms. Olsen, is that right?" he said, looking at me.

"Yes, that's me and this is Bronislawa Zakresevskis."

"Ah, yes, so it is. Now, Ms. Z, what do you know about the victim?"

About four minutes into Broni's monologue, the look on the detective's face was one of fading anticipation. He was beginning to realize Broni did not exactly know the identity or the origin of the dead man. She had given him a thorough grounding in the history and culture of the Livonian people. He was still holding out hope that somewhere in the travelogue there would emerge a tiny piece of useful information. He took advantage of a lull in the narrative. "So, am I to understand that you suspect the victim to be a Livonian based on the fact that he carried this coin?"

Broni looked at Crowley with an air of disbelief that he was not able to absorb the significance of what she had said. "Yes, Detective. There are not many people here in the township of East Gilmore that would have a bracteat."

Crowley looked at me. "Tell me again where you found this coin. What is it called?"

"Bracteat. It is a bracteat," I repeated, very proud of my ability to remember this since yesterday. "I found it on the sidewalk right in front of the office, kind of leaning up against the brick, just about where the body was."

"How do we know this belonged to the victim?" the detective asked.

"Well, it was right where he was found and according to Broni, a bracteat isn't something you run across every day. I've certainly never seen one there before."

"Yah, she is right. I have never seen a bracteat since I left home," Broni said. Home being the Latvian countryside, I assumed. Crowley didn't assume.

"Do you mean you haven't seen one since you left your house this morning or you haven't seen one since you arrived in the United States?"

"I haven't seen one since I left the house this morning," Broni answered, thus proving me wrong again. "I have a small collection of them that my grandmother gave me."

I looked at her. "You never told me you had these things at home."

"I don't tell people about them. I do not want the burglars to come."

"And you assumed I was going to round up a gang of ne'er-do-wells and raid your supply of bracteats?"

Detective Crowley seemed to be amused by this ludicrous exchange and I realized that Emma Peel would never have allowed herself to get embroiled in such a petty squabble.

"Broni, I just meant that when I found this thing yesterday, you never mentioned your collection. Maybe you dropped it on the way in to the office."

The ice-cold reindeer eyes showed just a flicker of uncertainty as they turned their gaze in my direction. "I most certainly did not drop it. My bracteats are well-contained."

At this the detective had to turn his head and fake a hacking cough. As soon as he regained his composure he asked, "Ms. Z, are you sure you didn't have any of them with you?"

"Yes, I know they are all at home. I have told you they are all contained in little boxes. I do not carry them about. As soon as I get home I will look at them to make sure."

Crowley stood up. "Thank you, ladies, for your information. We will certainly take this all into account during the investigation."

It appeared that we were being dismissed, so I stood up and Broni reluctantly followed suit.

At that point the door burst open and in came one of the cute little uniformed policemen that was at the office yesterday.

"This just came in on the fax machine," he said as he handed the detective a sheet of paper.

Bert Crowley started to read to himself. I thought we had better go, so I grabbed Broni's arm and started toward the door. It was a lot like dragging a reluctant elk. She dug her hooves in and didn't move very far.

"Just a minute, ladies. You might be interested in this. This is a report from Bob Hall, the coin dealer down on the corner of

Main and Wabash. He says the coin is a silver bracteat. I guess you were right, Ms. Z. He says that because it is silver, it most probably came from the Middle Ages. The earlier ones were gold. He also says that he has never seen one here in East Gilmore. He only sees them when he goes to New York to buy coins at big auctions."

He stood up behind his desk. "Ladies, I must ask you to keep this information to yourselves. If this coin did come from the victim, it could be important to not have the murderer know what we know. Also, Ms. Z, please look through your collection of these things very carefully. If you find any missing, let me know immediately." He handed her a card.

"Yes, sir, I will go and check my containers." Broni turned to face him and almost saluted. She was so happy to have been given a genuine police order.

Bert Crowley came around the desk and opened the door for us. He smiled and said "Good afternoon, ladies."

I could have sworn he was smiling directly at me but judging by the moony look on Broni's face, she thought he was smiling at her. He wasn't bad looking. Not that I paid much attention. He didn't look like John Steed. I doubt he owned an umbrella. He was tall, not real tall, just medium tall. Probably six foot one or two. Kind of thick graying hair. Probably about my age. We exited the office and walked down the hallway to the front door. Mindful every moment to make my walk one of perfect symmetry and grace in case Bert was still watching. Broni and I went out to her lumber wagon. I climbed up in the passenger's side. She started it up with a roar and we took off down the side street that would lead us back to Main Street and the office. I wondered if Bert Crowley had ever thought of having a crime-fighting partner dressed in black Spandex. This fantasy was cut short by Broni's sturdy size 12 walking shoe coming into sudden contact with the brake pedal. We were back at the office.

We walked in the door. I turned to go into my office. Broni followed me.

"What's the matter?" I said.

"I am worried about my bracteats. What if mine are stolen?"

"Run home and check. How long could it take?"

Broni looked more upset. "Hours. It could take hours. I have many containers."

"Hours? How many are there?"

"I think maybe four hundred," she said with a slightly sheepish look.

"Four hundred?" I sat down in my chair. "You told the detective it was a small collection. Where did you get four hundred of these things? It didn't sound like there were four hundred of them left in the whole world!"

"I have not mentioned them because I don't want people to know I have them. I told you that. My grandmother entrusted me with the family collections. The Zakreveskis have been collecting them since the beginning of the family," Broni said as she looked out the door. Larry Smith, the agent on duty, was sitting at the front desk within earshot.

"Broni, close the door. I don't want Larry hearing any of this." Larry was the office gossip. Actually one of several.

She stepped back to close the door and sat down.

I grabbed the calculator out of my purse. "You think you have about four hundred of these things?" She wobbled her head up and down.

I entered four hundred into the calculator. "And how much is each one worth?"

Broni thought for a moment. I could see the wheels turning behind the reindeer eyes.

"Some of them, like the later silver ones are worth about $75 each. The earlier gold ones are maybe $400. I don't have many of those."

She watched me punching numbers into the calculator. "What are you doing?"

"I am trying to figure out if you are sitting on a fortune." She looked horrified.

"No, I mean I am trying to see if your coins are worth a lot of money. If they are, it might not be safe for you to have them in your house. How many people know you have a major Livonian coin collection?"

She looked thoughtful. "Maybe only some cousins."

"Where are these cousins?"

"Mostly back in Latvia. There are two that came to the United States. They were not close to the rest of the family. They were talked about."

"Talked about? How were they talked about?"

"They may have been perpetrators of illegal activities."

"Broni, this is like pulling teeth. What kind of illegal things did they do?"

"We didn't know. People in the village talked about them. We thought at one time they may have been engaged in smuggling reindeer to Finland."

"Smuggling reindeer? Doesn't Finland have enough of its own? Is this like taking coals to Newcastle?"

I should have stopped while I was ahead. I had confused her with the Newcastle thing.

"Never mind. Forget I said that. We will assume Finland has an insatiable need for reindeer. Go ahead."

Broni nodded at me and continued, "There were some small villages along the border where the wolves had killed many of the reindeer and the people were too poor to pay much for new ones. So my cousins would steal reindeer and take them across the border and sell them for very little money."

"Reindeer rustlers? Taking from the rich and giving to the poor. That's like Robin Hood. Or Reindeer Hood in this case." I chuckled appreciatively at my rapier wit. "Your cousins were actually helping the poor people of Finland." I looked at Broni hopefully.

She shook her head. "No. It is not like that. The people they stole from were poor, too. They were only helping themselves. And they didn't even make much money at it."

"Why weren't they caught, if everyone knew what they were doing?"

"Some of them were. I have two cousins in prison there now, but two others escaped. Their mother heard from them after a couple of years. They were somewhere in California."

"Well, we know they are unemployed. I don't think reindeer smuggling is a big industry on the West Coast. There is no one else, no one locally that would know about these coins?"

"Yes, now there is. There is you and there is the detective."

"Ok, but nobody else?"

"I don't think so. It was a family secret back home. My mother and father had them until I became thirty years old. Then I got them because there was no male in the family to pass them on to."

"That wasn't yesterday. So, you've had them for twenty years? Where do you keep them? Wait, I don't really want to know all this stuff. It's just that probably Emma Peel would ask."

Broni looked very confused. I think it was the Emma Peel reference that threw her.

"Who is Emma Peel? Does she ask a lot of questions, too?"

"Yes, she does. She used to be on TV. A spy program."

That was a mistake. Broni perked up like a cat on a tuna boat.

"Tell me about the spies. Is it still on TV? Can I get it on cable?"

"You might be able to get it on DVD at Amazon or somewhere. Never mind that now, Broni. You need to go home and count your bracteats like the detective told you."

"I will do that tonight. It will take me some time. They are all in little containers with slots to hold each one."

"Can I help? What if I came over to your house tonight and we did it together?"

Her face lit up. "Oh, thank you, thank you. I can cook you supper, too."

"Oh, I don't want to put you to all that trouble. I have an appointment at 6, anyway, so I will just come over when I'm done."

I had eaten dinner at Broni's house once. I had indigestion for three days. I think it involved a lot of potatoes, flour, boiled peas and a quart of 10W30.

"Ok, I will get back to work. I will see you tonight. Thank you, thank you."

She opened the door and walked straight into Don, the office manager. He quickly took about six steps backward, looking for all the world like an arthropod doing the mambo.

"Oh, excuse me. I did not know you would be at the door," Broni said.

"No problem. I was just going to knock to see if you could come out here and help with some of the faxes that are coming in."

"Yes, I was waiting for them. They are from banks. I will get them now." Broni smiled at him as she sidled past, totally ignoring his feeble attempt at sarcasm.

Don looked puzzled at Broni's cooperative attitude. She knew a lot more than he did about the things coming over the fax machine, and if she had not been preoccupied with the problem of the upcoming bracteat census, they would have been taken care of in less time than it would take him to realize the fax machine was ringing.

He peeked into my office. "Is she ok?"

"Yes, Don, she's fine. She just had a personal problem she wanted to discuss. Very personal, you know, about, uh ..."

At that point his head disappeared from the doorway with a "Yeah, ok."

I didn't even have to make up any personal-sounding ailment. He was gone.

6 CHAPTER SIX

I wasn't telling a fib when I said I couldn't go to Broni's for dinner. I did have an appointment. It was for a listing on a very nice street in East Gilmore. I gathered up my contracts and disclosure forms and did a quick market analysis on the house.

On my way out the door, I went back to Broni's office. "I'll see you later. I'm going home to feed the boys and then go on my listing appointment."

She looked up and nodded. "Ok. Bye-bye."

I drove home thinking about this whole thing. The dead guy falls down outside our door. He drops a bracteat. Broni has bracteats. Can so many bracteats be a coincidence? Yesterday I didn't even know what a bracteat was. I was so preoccupied that I drove into the garage without even imagining the bushes rising to expose my secret car park.

The boys were waiting in the kitchen as usual.

"It's only 4:30. Please find something to do between now and supper time." Ira looked up and meowed indignantly, as if I were questioning his internal clock. They both marched off to sit in the living room. I checked the answering machine. Nothing but hang-ups. Probably the talent department at M-G-M not wanting to leave a message. The postman must have sorted my mail, taking out the good stuff. All he left me were bills. I threw them down on the hall table and went up the stairs to the computer room in the back of the house. It had been my older son's room before he grew up and moved out. Now it had three desks, two computers and assorted printers. I sat down and turned one of the computers on. Leaning back in the chair, I shut my eyes and tried to make a picture in my head connecting the dead guy, bracteats, Broni, Latvia, Livonia and anything else I could think of. Nothing was forming. There weren't enough dots to connect to make a picture. Or else my detective skills were not what I imagined them to be. Maybe picturing myself in black Spandex is not enough. Maybe Emma Peel had some actual talent or training or something that I don't have, in addition to a body that can fit into black Spandex. I checked my e-mail. Nothing there either, except an ad for chest enlargement herbs. They obviously know nothing about target marketing.

"Let's go get supper," I yelled as I started toward the stairs. Two big gray fur balls beat me down the stairs and tore through the rooms to the kitchen. I fed them their can of little beef squares. That stuff doesn't smell bad. I wonder what it tastes like. I may find out one of these days. I figured I had better get myself something to eat, too, so that I could honestly refuse Broni's Livonian cuisine. I fixed a salad and sat down to read this morning's paper. An article about the dead guy was on the local news page. Nothing we didn't already know. In fact, we knew more than they did, since the information about the bracteat had not been released.

I put my salad bowl in the dishwasher, ran back upstairs to brush my teeth and hair and went off to the appointment.

I pulled up in front of the house on Southampton Court. It was a beautiful three-story Tudor, 4,400 square feet, seven bedrooms, four full baths, two half baths, in-ground pool surrounded by gardens, a three-car garage and a big lot. I got out of the car, retrieved my briefcase and started up the front walk. The door was answered by a distinguished-looking elderly gentleman.

"How do you do? I am Ophelia Olsen from Village Realty." He looked up at my hair and down at my shoes and everywhere in between. It was at that moment I realized I had worn my shoes with the tiny little hole in the left big toe area. He had probably spotted it. It's not easy to miss size elevens.

I must have passed inspection, albeit minimally, because he finally stepped back a little and said, "Come in."

I took a couple steps into the foyer and looked up. It was two stories high with a great 1920s iron chandelier hanging from the ceiling. On my right the staircase started its ascent with five steps, then it took a left turn at the first landing and went up another nine, then another turn to reach the second floor. All done in quarter sawn oak with a dark stain.

"I am Alfred Fitch. Please come in."

I followed Alfred into a room that had to be about 35 feet long by 25 feet wide with a light-gray marble fireplace at one end and a row of windows looking out onto a garden. Under one of the windows there was a sofa about eight feet long. On the couch was a life-sized dried-apple doll. Mr. Fitch walked over to the couch and turned to me.

"Miss Olsen, I would like you to meet Mrs. Fitch."

The dried-apple doll's face cracked open and exposed two little brown stubs. A dried-apple smile.

I'm sure Emma Peel would have recovered her composure faster than I did. Also, I had to remember I was not in Emma Peel mode this evening.

"It's so nice to meet you, Mrs. Fitch. What a lovely home you and your husband have here."

"He's dead." Mrs. Fitch creaked out the words just about how a dried apple would sound.

In times of stress and/or confusion my mind kind of runs around grabbing at thoughts and trying to assemble them into something that makes sense. It was doing that right now. Mr. Fitch didn't look dead. Well, actually he did look dead, not taking into account the fact that he was walking and talking. Apparently the strain of all the thinking started to show on my face because Mr. Fitch broke in with an explanation.

"Ms. Olsen. She means that her husband is dead. I am her son. She is my mother."

Ok, now I was having another brain attack. If she was his mother, she had to be the same age as a Philadelphia sideboard. Come to think of it, Alfred resembled a dried fig. Perhaps the entire family was composed of desiccated fruit.

"Oh, I'm sorry, it's just that you look so young!" I babbled in an attempt to recover my savoir faire.

The split in the dried-apple face grew wider. "Ms. Olsen, you're flustered."

I gave up and just stood there and smiled. "I'm sorry."

"Don't be sorry. Nobody expects and old fart like Alfred to still have a mother. I'll be 102 on my next birthday."

"Congratulations. That's quite a feat."

"Bullroar. That's no feat. For some reason I just haven't died yet, and you're not making any points here. I'm really only 84. Alfred, show her the house. Let's see how much money we can get out of this place. Just remember, Ms. what's-your-name, it better be a lot."

So Alfred is only a few years older than I am, unless his mother was a child bride. When I first came in I thought he was elderly, if I remember correctly. I guess other people with gray hair look older than I think I do. I decided my best course of action would be to just do what I know how to do, which is look at houses. I followed Alfred out of the cavernous living room into the equally cavernous dining room, through the butler's pantry, the kitchen, and the sun porch. One impression stood out. Everything was of very high quality and very old. We then descended into the bowels of the house. A long stairway past walls made from local red sandstone led to the uneven concrete floor. Straight ahead was a boiler that looked to be approximately the same size as the ones on the Titanic and about the same age.

"We have the boiler serviced every spring and every fall," Alfred volunteered.

"Very good. Maintenance is so important," I burbled in my best professional voice. I was wondering how old the serviceman was. The new furnace people wouldn't even recognize this thing.

"The boiler service people have been with us a long time. The last man said it was quite efficient for its age."

I was wondering how efficient the serviceman was.

"Here is the hot water tank. It was replaced about six years ago." Alfred smiled in its direction. He appeared to be quite fond of it. Maybe it's the only thing he's ever seen that's less than 100 years old.

"Thank you, Mr. Fitch. I think I just need to see the rest of the house and ask you a few questions and I'll be done." I started toward the stairway, quite proud of myself for maintaining my professional demeanor and not yet having tripped over anything. Just then my foot caught a pile of fur and I skidded sideways, smacking my right hip into the stone wall. I looked down to see what appeared to be an old gray mop with a cloud of dust rising from where my foot struck it.

"Oh, be careful, Miss Olsen, don't fall. I really should move him. That's Mopsy, Mother's last poodle. He died about four years ago."

"My, he's in remarkable shape, considering."

"Yes, the dry air caused him to become desiccated and preserved quite nicely."

Emma Peel notwithstanding, I had a terrible urge to get the hell out of there. I started toward the stairs again, watching the floor very carefully for any signs of pet remains.

Alfred followed me to the top of the stairs, flipping light switches off. We went back through the living room.

Alfred stopped to speak to his mother. "Mother, please let me dispose of Mopsy. Miss Olsen tripped over him and nearly hurt herself."

"That's because she's a clumsy cow. Mopsy's not going anywhere until I do. I want him buried with me like those Egyptian queens did with their dogs."

I thought the ancient Egyptians were fonder of cats than dogs, but I did not think this was a good time to start an argument.

Alfred turned to me with a pained expression on his face. "Let me show you the second floor."

I followed him with as much dignity as I could muster after having been referred to as a bovine creature. And a clumsy one at that. I could feel the power of suggestion affecting my gait. I could even feel my udder swinging.

As we went up the stairs, I looked at my watch. I needed to get through here in the next few minutes to have some time to help Broni tonight. We came to a large landing at the top of the staircase. Alfred proceeded to show me five bedrooms and three bathrooms. The largest room belonging to Mother. All done in wallpaper from the late 1930s, with a few cobwebs from the same era. We weren't done yet. The third floor had another two bedrooms and full bath. Then we started down. As we reached the first floor again, I thought it only civilized to say good night to Mrs. Fitch, even though her opinion of my grace was less than optimal.

"Good night, Mrs. Fitch. I will be calling within a day or two to schedule another appointment after I've completed my market analysis."

"It better be a good one or I'll call those people down the street from you." The apple grin showed up again.

As Alfred showed me to the door, I asked him about any improvements or maintenance to the house.

"Do you mean like a new bathroom or new roof or something like that?" he asked.

"Yes, exactly."

"Well, Mother doesn't like to spend money on those things until it's absolutely necessary. The roof is inspected every year. It's slate and not likely to wear out. The built-in refrigeration units in the kitchen are inspected every year by the same company that does the boiler. Everything is in very good condition."

Why am I not surprised that the same ancient company that does the boiler does the refrigerator? Why can't I get the easy listings? Why don't I stop asking myself questions and just leave?

"I will finish my market analysis and get back to you in a day or so, Mr. Fitch. I understand you are anxious to get your house on the market. Do you and your mother have other living arrangements yet?"

"I have some thoughts on that, but we may need you to help us. Goodnight, Miss Olsen."

I stepped outside the door. "Goodnight, Mr. Fitch."

As I drove away from the town's first Dried Fruit Museum, I wondered what Mr. Fitch had in mind for his mother's future living arrangements. When I come back there may be two old gray lumps on the basement floor. I will have to ponder that later. Right now, I needed to get to Broni's house to help her with the bracteat enumeration.

She lived in a small house that her parents bought after they had been in this country a few years. It was on the outskirts of the village, in a small, primarily working-class community. All the houses were clean and neat, but none so much as Broni's. I swear she must wash the siding on a weekly basis. I stopped here last summer and she was up on the roof with a broom.

Several leaves had had the audacity to land on the shingles. Fortunately it was a small house and the roof could be swept in a matter of minutes, should one have that desire.

I pulled into the driveway and went around to the side door. Broni was already opening it.

"I saw you coming down the street. Come in. I have some of my reindeer cookies for you." She beamed as she held out a plate heaped up with about two hundred cookies.

These I will eat. I have had them before and they are very good. The "reindeer" in the name does not refer to an ingredient, but rather the shape. She cuts them out with a reindeer-shaped cookie cutter. I am not sure why. They would taste the same even if they were not little reindeer. That is my opinion. She is convinced something would happen to the flavor if she did not make them the same shape that her grandmother did. In fact, the cookie cutter she used belonged to her grandmother and probably her grandmother's grandmother. It was handmade of tin and the joint was soldered, probably with lead solder which may have contributed to some of her family's eccentricities.

I took about six cookies (hey, I'm a growing girl) and followed Broni into the living room. She had all the shades drawn and the curtains shut. She wasn't taking any chances. On the long coffee table were spread out about forty or fifty plastic boxes. They had covers on them and it looked like little slots inside holding up coins. These were the famous bracteat containers. She sat down on the couch and picked up a box to show me. I took it and sat down. The little bracteats were lined up like Necco wafers.

"See, this box has ten bracteats. Each one is a little different, so they are from a different year or time period. They did not make a new one every year, so the same one maybe was used for a few years," she explained.

"So, what are the numbers for?"

"That is to put the boxes in chronological order, as best I can. It is not easy to date a bracteat."

I wouldn't know. I hadn't dated anything in a long time, say nothing about a bracteat. Enough about my social life.

"Ok, how do we check them? Are all the boxes supposed to have ten coins in them?"

"Yes, all except the last one, which has only five. We have to look in each box carefully, so as not to let them fall out." She looked at me as if she rather expected me to be clumsy enough to dump the whole collection on the floor. She was wrong. I dropped only one box. I thought she was going to call the Livonian KGB or whatever they have. I dived for the coins and caught a couple of them before they even hit the floor. The rest I scooped up and put on the table, while looking at Broni with a rather sheepish grin.

"I'm sorry, I guess I dropped them. I'll put them back in the box."

"I will put them in the box." I thought I detected just a teensy bit of hostility in her voice.

"Ok, I will just look at the next box." I picked it up very carefully. "Say, this won't take long at all. We can just look in each box and see if there are any empty slots, right?"

"No. We have to make sure there are no empty slots and also check the back of each coin to see if the tiny sticker is there. Then we will know if someone put a counterfeit in there."

I wanted to ask if there was a big business in counterfeiting coins that hadn't been used in a hundred years, but figured I was in enough trouble already. So I looked in the box to determine the number of coins and I dutifully turned the box around to look at the backs and find the little stickers. I already had been warned about unnecessarily touching the coins. Something about the oil in the skin that could affect the patina. Fortunately we could see the backs without touching them because of the way the little boxes were made.

After about an hour of this, we were down to the last box. Broni picked it up and looked inside. There were five coins.

"See, it is true. None of them is missing. There are five in here."

"Ok, we had better tell Detective Crowley. But I guess it can wait until morning."

Broni got up off the couch and went to her desk. She picked up a business card. "Here is his phone number."

"You can call him in the morning when you get to the office. If you want me to, I will, but right now it is late, I am tired and I want to go home and go to bed."

"Thank you, Oph, for helping me look at them."

I walked to the door. "No problem, Broni. I'm just glad they're all there. See you in the morning."

7 CHAPTER SEVEN

Morning dawned as usual, at dawn. My TV set went on at seven a.m. Plenty early to wake up, I think. Unfortunately, that's not what woke me up. It was a gray furry face right in mine, yelling for his breakfast. This happened the first time at 5:30. Way too early to wake up unless you have chickens to milk or some such early-morning activity. Shutting my eyes tightly let me doze off for a few minutes at a time, but it was a rather disturbed hour and a half during which I could have been sleeping soundly. A fact of which I informed Ira as soon as I could keep my eyes open for any length of time. He pretty much ignored my lecture by keeping up his line of chirpings and chatterings. So, we had another talk about rudely interrupting people while they are talking and/or trying to sleep.

During all this I had risen from my bed, bathed, dressed, performed my extensive beauty ritual - alas, to no avail - and descended the stairs. The sunlight streamed in through the tall living room windows and I could see the little bright green leaves coming out on the crabapple tree. Spring is one of my favorite times of the year. I love the green leaves and blue sky and red and pink flowers. It looks like the earth finally woke up after a long winter. We did breakfast. A can of salmon for the Gershwin brothers and my pills and a glass of water for me.

I gathered my bag full of file folders and collected my purse, then set them right back down again and turned and went into the dining room. My mother's piano was in there. I suppose I should call it my piano now. It has been here for nearly twenty years. The piano is good for shutting out the rest of the world. I sat down and looked at the sheet music for Brahms' Piano Sonata No. 1 in C Major. Looking at it usually turns out far better than my attempting to play it. Unfortunately for music lovers everywhere, I decided to begin. As the first resounding chords echoed through the house, Ira jumped up on the piano stool. He is, at the moment, the only inhabitant of the house that truly appreciates my piano playing. George seems to keep his distance. Perhaps that is the influence of his human counterpart.

Anyway, I stumbled my way through the first three pages with Ira sitting quietly by my side. I stopped playing and looked down at him.

"I suppose that is enough for this morning. I really should get to the office. Broni will be trying to call Detective Crowley, and I am on floor duty. Maybe when I get home I will play some more."

Ira emitted a grateful chirp. I think he was grateful for the promise of more music later. Or just grateful that I had stopped playing. He didn't say which.

I pulled into my parking space in front of the office. Broni was at the reception desk, shuffling through the big books containing all the listings for the office. Through the window I could see her sticking new pages in and taking out old ones. I gathered my bags out of the back seat and walked in the door. I didn't think much about the sidewalk being formerly occupied by a dead guy. I guess we were all getting used to it.

"Hi, Broni. Did you call the detective yet and tell him all your bracteats were intact?"

"No. I did not. I wonder if you will do it for me. I don't want to confuse him."

Good idea, I thought to myself. Between Broni's English and her TV-cop vocabulary, who knows what message he might get.

"Alright, I'll call him. Do you have his card handy?" She shook her head up and down and walked down the hallway toward her desk. I followed. I had to admit to myself that I was not averse to the idea of calling the semi-handsome detective. Perhaps he saw in me the latent Emma Peel that others had difficulty perceiving. I'd better keep in touch frequently so he will have the opportunity to fantasize about me in black Spandex.

Broni fished around in her giant knit bag until she found the card. She had knitted the bag herself. Her grandmother had taught her to make these traditional Livonian folk purses. It wasn't really a purse, but a bag in which women of the town carried everything. They went to the market and took food home in it; they carried baked goods to the neighbors in it; they carried babies in it (both human and reindeer); they picked up dried reindeer chips off the ground in the fields and took them home to burn in the stoves, and probably a whole lot of other things she has neglected to tell me. Surprisingly enough, she could always find things in there. There must be some kind of bizarre filing system inside the woven-yarn satchel. Of course, in the old country, they used reindeer fur spun into yarn. Here, in the U.S., she was forced to use either wool or man-made yarns. This did not go over well. She couldn't understand why there were no yarn shops that would sell her reindeer yarn.

"Thanks. I think I'll make a copy of this. I guess I lost the one he gave me." I took the card in to the computer room and put it on the copy machine.

"How did you do on that listing appointment last night, Oph?" I jumped, startled by the voice behind me. It was Don, the office manager.

"Oh, I think pretty well. They are a slightly strange family. The house is high quality and well-maintained."

"How much are you going to put on it?"

"I don't know yet. I haven't had a chance to finish the market analysis. I think it will probably be around 260 or 270."

"Okey-dokey, just make sure you get that listing. We need more inventory. That would be a good one to advertise. It's in the best neighborhood in town and the Fitches could provide some good referral business. They were one of the first families in the village. Mrs. Fitch's father-in-law started the iron foundry over by the river."

I knew the Fitch family connection to local industry, but I couldn't imagine the Fitches having any contemporaries to refer me to. Mrs. Fitch's last contemporary went down on the Lusitania.

"I'm going to get it done today. I told them I'd get back to them in a day or two. Mrs. Fitch said if the price wasn't high enough she'd list with Fred Ford's company."

Don's face was split by his slightly oily "you'd-better-get-the-listing" smile. I looked back at the copy machine and took the card out.

"I'll do the best I can with it," I told him, "but I'm not going to artificially inflate it just to get the listing. I think these people are going to be a little tough to work with. Especially Mother Fitch."

"Don't forget, Oph, they are among the first families of East Gilmore and are very important here."

"Ok. I'll keep that in mind, Don," I said as I wondered how well the news of a dead dog in the basement would go over with the Daughters of the American Revolution. I wasn't sure that Mrs. Fitch belonged to the DAR. On the other hand, Mrs. Fitch probably attended elementary school with Martha Washington and that alone would keep her membership in good standing.

I gave Broni back Detective Crowley's business card and went to my desk. I did need to get that market analysis done for the Fitches. Don was right about one thing. It would be a good listing. Hopefully I could get it done today and meet with them this evening. I called the police station. Crowley was out so I left a message on his voice mail. Drat. I wanted to use my potentially Emma Peel-like voice on him live, instead of a recording.

I started pulling up comparable properties in the Fitches' neighborhood and figuring out a fair price for that monstrous house, minus the deceased creature in the basement.

About two hours later, I looked up to see a large blonde head taking up much of my doorway.

"Hi, Broni. Need something?"

"Ya. I just got a telephone call from Detective Crowley. He wants to talk to me. Will you go with me?"

"Of course. When?"

"He says as soon as possible."

"Ok, let's go. Can I drive this time?" I said, my selfish survival instinct surfacing.

"Ya, I will get my bag." She lumbered off to fetch the satchel.

Don stuck his head in my door. "How're you doing on that listing?"

"Almost done. I just have to run out to drive past a couple of comps. Be back shortly."

Broni came along and we both took off out the door before he could ask any more questions. As we were getting into my car, Mr. Bosch was coming down the sidewalk. We waved. He lifted his hand in a brief greeting and hurried on his way.

"He hasn't been in for coffee in a couple of days, has he?"

Broni shook her head from side to side. "No, not since the day of the dead guy."

"The Day of the Dead Guy? Is this an official day now? I would much prefer a more cheerful holiday to remember in the future."

Broni just looked out the window. I guess she was accustomed to my flights of out-of-mindedness.

I pulled up to the police station and turned into the parking lot. We went in and stood in front of the desk sergeant. The same one as before. As he looked up, a spark of unpleasant recognition flew through his eyes. He didn't speak.

"Good afternoon, Sergeant." I said.

"Yes, good afternoon to you, Sergeant," Broni piped up. "I am Bronislawa Zakreveskis. Detective Crowley has summoned me here to speak to him."

The sergeant looked slightly askance at us while he was dialing Crowley's office.

"Detective, two ladies to see you. One says you wanted to see her. Ok, right away." He hung up the phone and looked at us.

"You can go right in," he said.

Broni wasted no time trotting down the hall way and rapping smartly on Crowley's door. The door opened and Broni walked in just as I caught up with her. Holding the door for us was Hubert Crowley, the not-half-bad-looking detective.

"Good afternoon, ladies," he said in a reasonably attractive voice. Not too deep, yet containing no falsetto tones. A good sign.

"Hello to you, sir. How may I assist you?" Broni must have watched another CSI marathon last night.

Crowley tried to conceal a little smile. "Thank you for coming Ms. Z, and you too, Ms. Olsen."

Ms. Olsen? Doesn't he recognize Emma Peel? Maybe I should change my tactics. Perhaps I could borrow Superman's idea and have an everyday identity along with my secret crime-fighting persona. So for now I remain Ms. Olsen. Only during a moment of intense investigation will I reveal my true identity and rip off these ordinary clothes to expose the Spandex and those pointy-toed boots. Criminal investigation, that is. Let's keep our mind on our business ...

"Ms. Olsen, excuse me ..."

I focused on my immediate surroundings to find Crowley and Broni staring at me.

"Oh, I'm sorry, my mind must have wandered. What did you ask?"

"Ms. Olsen, I asked if you agreed with Ms. Z that all the coins were present in her collection"

"Oh, yes. We looked through all the boxes and there were no empty spots. They were all there." I smiled at him to alleviate any doubts about my mental health. I'm not sure it had the intended effect. He shook his head almost imperceptibly in my direction and turned back to Broni.

"Ms. Z, you say you did not recognize the deceased, is that right?"

"Yes, sir. I do not ever remember seeing him before that day." Broni sat up very straight.

Crowley looked thoughtful for a minute, then spoke. "I have been contacted by the Latvian Embassy in Washington."

Broni perked right up if that's possible, since she was pretty perked already.

Crowley continued. "I am going to tell you ladies something that you need to keep absolutely quiet. You cannot tell anyone without endangering the progress and possible success of this investigation. Is that understood?"

Broni's head bobbed up and down like one of those little plastic dogs that people put up in the back window of their cars. I thought I could hear something rattling.

"Ms. Olsen, do you understand?"

I was taken aback. Did he think that the alter ego of one of the world's great criminal chasers and wearer of Spandex would not understand the need for secrecy? I was insulted.

"Yes, I completely understand. I will not say a word." Come to think of it, maybe he's not so good-looking.

"Good. The attaché of military affairs has asked us to look into the disappearance of one of their operatives. He was sent here on an investigation and has not been heard from in a few days. I told him about our unidentified corpse and they sent a picture to see if he might be their missing man. He is. The county coroner's office has confirmed that he died of a severe blow to the head. He probably never saw it coming. It would have been very quick and very hard. We do not know how probable it is that this was accidental. Our investigation is continuing to treat this as a possible homicide."

At the word "'operative," we both leaned forward a little. Now, this is right up Emma Peel's alley. In spite of my fantasies, I was still just a real estate agent sitting here with the office secretary. I wasn't sure how we fit in to all this.

"The morning I found the body, you were looking at a big chunk of icicle in the parking lot. I thought it may possibly have been an accident that the icicle fell and hit him," I postulated.

"We considered that, but in reconstructing the scenario, it seems unlikely that it was an accident. But, you are right, anything is possible."

"How can we help you?" I asked, not sure of our - or at least my - function here.

Broni scowled at me, as if I had spoiled her chances of getting in on real police work. My Emma Peel fantasies were fading fast in the light of running into a real, live murderer. I really just wanted the Spandex and champagne.

"Miss Z, I would like to ask for your help. I don't know all the details yet. The attaché is going to be sending me more information on the investigation that this man was working on. It may involve some other Latvian nationals. This is where we need your help."

"Yes, I will help as well as I can. What shall I do?" Broni bounced in her chair.

"I know from our previous conversations that you are acquainted with most of the members of the Latvian families in the village. Is that correct?"

Broni's head bounced up and down in the affirmative.

"I am going to ask you to keep your eyes and ears open. We are looking for strangers in town. If you should hear or see anything that would lead us to the presence of these people, I need you to call me immediately."

"Yes, sir. I will do that."

"Now Ms. Olsen. Since you work with Ms. Z, I would like you to be aware of what I have asked her to do. If you could be of any help to her we would appreciate it."

"Of course. I'll help her all I can. We can keep our eyes and ears busy. How many of these people are there?"

"We don't know. It would only take one to commit a murder. Can I count on both of you to keep this completely confidential?"

Broni answered. "Yes. We will be completely quiet. We will not tell anyone what we are doing. We will find these people."

"Wait, I need to make something else very clear. I do not want you to 'find them.' I just want you to report anything that might be helpful to us. Do you understand? I do not want you chasing, following, or in any way getting anywhere near this person or persons. Just very calmly report to me anything suspicious. I do not want you tipping off anyone nor putting yourselves in danger."

This man obviously was blind to my hidden talents. All of them.

"Yes, Detective, we will be the souls of discretion. I will make sure Broni doesn't get any ideas about single-handedly apprehending any Latvian criminals."

He looked at me as if he were sorry he had deputized us. I knew Broni was disappointed in not being asked to run the streets armed with some kind of criminal-bashing device, but she would follow instructions. I began to think this could be interesting. After all, the criminal wouldn't know I was observing him, or her, so I would be safe. I would remain in my everyday disguise so they couldn't put the finger on me as a detective type. Broni and I could see a certain number of people as they passed by the office every day and maybe actually find these evildoers.

I looked up to find the two of them staring at me again.

"Yes, we can do this," I babbled, hoping I hadn't been asked a question during my moment away from them.

"Good," Crowley said. "Just remember, neither one of you is to approach or contact any suspicious people. Understand?"

"We understand. Don't worry, we aren't that brave," I volunteered, hoping Broni agreed with me. "What did these people do? Do you think they murdered the operative?"

"We don't know that. The gentleman I spoke with this morning emphasized the fact that this is an ongoing investigation and all information is confidential. Any security breach could jeopardize the outcome. That's all I can tell you." He handed each of us another business card. "Keep these cards with you. My cell phone number is written on the back. Call me anytime you see anything out of the ordinary."

He stood up. We stood up. He smiled. I gave him one of my most alluring smiles. It didn't seem to have much effect. In fact, I am not sure he even saw it. He was opening the door for us. "Have a good day, ladies."

We walked out past the desk sergeant whose face reflected the relief he felt to see us go.

Out we went into the sunshine. Broni was silent. She opened the passenger-side door on my car and plumped down on the seat. I got in and started the car. I looked over at her.

"What's the matter?"

"I have many questions. What was this man investigating? It must be something quite bad for him to be killed because of it, and it is classified information."

"It's hard to believe that something like this has happened in our little village, and now to find out it is connected to something bigger is even harder to believe. Do you suppose this is some kind of international intrigue?"

"You mean like 'The Third Man'?" she said.

"Yeah, something like that." I drove out of the parking lot back toward the office. It took us about a minute longer to get there when I was driving.

Larry was still at the front desk. "You ladies have a nice lunch?"

"Yes, Larry, very nice. What's been going on here?"

"I put a Mr. Fitch through to your voice mail."

"Oh, blammity, I've got to get that done."

I went back into my office and worked some more on the market analysis for the Fitches' property.

Another forty-five minutes and it was done. I called the house. Mr. Fitch answered. "Hello, Mr. Fitch, this is Ophelia Olsen. I have your market analysis done. I would like to come and talk to you about listing your house. Would sometime this evening be convenient?"

Mr. Fitch was amenable to my going over there about seven p.m. That will be good; I can get this one wrapped up and on the market. Hopefully it will sell fast so I can make enough money for another mortgage payment on my own house. A roof over your head is a good thing.

8 CHAPTER EIGHT

The rest of the day passed uneventfully. I finished up everything I needed for the listing appointment this evening. About three o'clock I decided to go home. I wanted to stop at the little discount market on the way. I could use some food in the house. I think the freezer had six ice cream suckers and a pork chop that was borderline in terms of age.

I left my office and walked down the hall. I poked my head around the corner toward Broni's desk.

"Bye. I'm leaving now. I'll see you tomorrow."

She looked up from the file drawer.

"Ok. Thank you for going with me to the police station."

"No problem. Why were you afraid? I thought you were an expert on police procedure."

"I watch many TV programs and learn from them, but having dead bodies and murderers on our doorstep is much more serious."

"Oh, don't worry. The police will catch whoever did this. Besides, they must have targeted that man. That wasn't just a random killing, according to what the detective said. He was sent here to investigate something. So, he must have gotten too close to whatever those people didn't want him to find out. They don't care about us."

"What if they find out that we are supposed to watch for

them?"

"How are they going to find out? We are just supposed to watch from a distance and not go anywhere near them. We may never even see them. You may be able to find out something through some of your friends and just tell the detective. See. It's simple."

Her big blue reindeer eyes looked a little worried. "Ok. I will not worry about it. I will just try to do what the detective said."

"Good girl. See you tomorrow."

I went back down the hallway toward the front door.

"When are you seeing the Fitches?" a voice emanating from the manager's office said.

I stuck my head in. "Tonight. I talked to Mr. Fitch a little while ago."

"Good, good. Just make sure you impress them."

"Yeah, ok. See you tomorrow."

Impress them? With what? Maybe I could learn how to juggle or turn somersaults in the living room. That would impress them. Especially when my somersault sent me crashing into the T'ang dynasty vase on the sideboard. Boy, would they be impressed.

I got into my car and took off for the grocery store. I picked up a bag of frozen chicken and some lettuce. That will do for a few days.

The Gershwin brothers were waiting at the kitchen door.

"Hello, George; hello, Ira. It's not supper time yet."

I put down my purse and grocery bags. Ira was right up on the table trying to see into the bag.

"There's nothing in here for you today. Go take a nap and let me put the food away."

Ira looked up and chirped. I think it was a chirp of displeasure.

I had a couple of hours before my appointment, so I decided some yard work would be a good idea. Somebody had better do it and the Gershwin brothers were too short to push the snow shovel.

It took just until dinnertime to rake and do some cleaning up after the melting snow and put the tools away. I went back into the house to find the boys waiting at the door.

"Ok. Now it's supper time. What flavor do you want tonight?"

Ira chirped and George just looked like he would rather eat any flavor than answer my stupid questions.

"Beef and liver, it is." After feeding them, I got a bowl of lettuce out of the refrigerator. I took a closer look at it. It was brown. Time for the new lettuce.

About twenty to seven, I decided it was time to go. I had all my paperwork ready and changed back into my office clothes. I set off to impress the Fitches.

I drove down the tree-lined side streets and made a left turn onto Southampton Court. I pulled up in front of number 396. I didn't dare park in the driveway without being invited. I was afraid Mrs. Fitch would come out and bite a chunk out of my tire, now that Flopsy or Mopsy wasn't around to do it.

I reluctantly got out of my car. I didn't have a lot of confidence about this appointment. I stood up straight and realized I would be an embarrassment to Emma Peel. She wouldn't be frightened of an old lady. I strode resolutely to the door and rang the bell.

The door was opened by Mr. Fitch. "Good evening, Miss Olsen. Please come in." He stepped back to let me pass by.

"It's nice to see you again, Mr. Fitch. How are you?"

"Very well, thank you. Please come into the dining room. We'll be able to look at your report there."

"Certainly," I said as I followed him through the living room. I glanced at the couch but there was no dried-apple figure.

I went through the tall archway into the dining room and discovered the dried-apple face at the end of the table. Mr.

Fitch had already reached the end of the table and stood behind a chair beside his mother. He motioned for me to sit on the other side of Mother. "Please have a seat, Miss Olsen."

"Thank you. Good evening, Mrs. Fitch. How are you this evening?"

"How the hell did you expect me to be? Every bone in my body hurts and I'm constipated." She punctuated that statement by emitting a short but powerful belch.

"I'm sorry to hear that." Bad choice of words. "Let me show you the market analysis on your property."

I opened my folder and proceeded to explain how I gathered information on comparable properties in the neighborhood and used them to arrive at a reasonable sale price for their house. I had taken pictures of the others and done what I thought was a bang-up job on the presentation.

"After considering the comparable sale prices, I think your house will sell somewhere between two hundred sixty-five and two hundred seventy-five thousand dollars. I would suggest the initial list price be two hundred seventy-nine thousand." I relaxed a little and leaned back in my chair ever so slightly, thinking I had done the best I could. Now to see the reaction.

"Horse hockey. This house is worth three-fifty if it's worth a penny," Mrs. Fitch spit out through the hole between the wrinkles.

Mr. Fitch bowed his head slightly, then looked up and said, "Thank you, Miss Olsen. That was very thorough job. Perhaps you could explain in a little more detail how you arrived at that figure. Mother seems to disagree."

"Yes, certainly. When I look at the other properties, I take the sale prices and make adjustments to them based on the differences between those houses and yours. Mrs. Fitch, you are correct that some houses here in the neighborhood have sold in the mid-three hundreds, with one selling just under four hundred thousand. However I had to look at those prices and then adjust. For example, the house that sold for just under four hundred had a brand new sixty-thousand-dollar kitchen, three completely updated full baths, a reproduction of an English pub in the basement. All the interior wall surfaces were new and so were the boilers, hot water tanks and much of the plumbing."

The dried-apple face seemed to start twitching sideways around the hole in the middle, while the nose was bobbing up and down. I think she was sputtering. Finally some words emerged. "Do you mean to tell me you put more stock in all that new stuff than you do in the original?"

I figured I was in a pretty big bind here. I may as well go for the reality check.

"Mrs. Fitch, I can understand how you feel. Unfortunately, neither you nor I set the sale price on the house. The market does. The house will bring only what someone is willing to pay for it. Many of the buyers who have the income to purchase a house in this price range are young professionals with two people in the family working. They have neither the time nor the interest in keeping up the original equipment. For example, they would prefer to put in a new boiler that is far more efficient and easier to maintain than the old one, no matter how good it was when it was new. Same goes for the kitchen equipment, the laundry and the hot water tanks. There is a good chance that someone would want or need to update much of the plumbing. The electrical system was not designed for the load placed upon it by today's lifestyle. We have computers, blow dryers, clothes dryers, microwaves, toaster ovens, wide-screen televisions, stereo equipment and a whole lot more. I just cannot compare this house equally with that other one. Two seventy-nine is a reasonable starting price, but you need to be prepared to negotiate. It will probably sell a little lower."

I sat back in my chair again, aware of the fact that I had been leaning forward and getting louder as the speech progressed.

Mr. and Mother Fitch were both staring at me. I assumed the next thing I would hear was one or both of them asking me to leave. I thought I had pretty well cooked my goose with this one. I started to gather up my papers.

"That house only sold for that much because that besotted old fool bought it," Mrs. Fitch growled.

Mr. Fitch looked at his mother. "Now, Mother, Robert just wanted a nicer home for his new bride."

"That's what I said. He's got the hots for some bimbo young enough to be his daughter."

"Mother, Miss Olsen probably isn't interested in the neighbors' lives."

On the contrary, this sounded more interesting than anything else I'd heard tonight. "Oh, do you know the gentleman who bought 425 Southampton?"

"Yes, he's one of Alfred's golfing buddies. He has a vacuum cleaner store in the village. He lived about six houses down that way, now he's spent almost four hundred thousand dollars on a house for a bride that isn't ever going to show up."

"Mother, I think we'd better get back to business and not hold Miss Olsen up."

I think I would rather have pumped Mother for more information than gone back to business, but I did want to get home eventually.

"Miss Olsen, what you have told us tonight makes a lot of sense. As much as we love this house, you were absolutely right about many things. It does need updating and I can understand your point about the price. Mother, what do you think?"

Mother Fitch looked as though she could spit tacks out of the sides of her mouth. I just hoped she had a lousy aim. The mouth kind of chewed a little and the eyes tried to bore a hole right through my forehead. Finally she spoke. "All right. Let me sign the papers and get it over with. You sound like you know what you're talking about, but I still don't have to like it. You'd better sell this place fast, Missy."

A claw-like appendage crawled up onto the table from out of her long sleeve.

"Give me a pen."

I handed her the pen and showed her where to sign, then pushed the papers over to Alfred.

They signed the rest of the forms with little conversation. I put them back in my folder and said, "Thank you. I don't think you'll be disappointed. I will do my best to sell your house in as short a time as possible. I'll put the sign up tomorrow and the first ad will be in the newspaper next weekend."

Mother wiggled sideways in her chair as though she were trying to stand up. "Alfred, get me to the couch. My behind hurts. This blabbermouth went on so long, my bones are killing me."

Alfred helped his mother up and walked her into the living room where she plopped on the couch. I waited in the dining room for him to come back. I didn't know if they would approve of me going to the front door unaccompanied.

"Miss Olsen, thank you for your patience with Mother."

"You're most welcome, Mr. Fitch. I hope she will be happy with the results."

"Oh, she won't be happy with anything, Miss Olsen. But that isn't your fault. Please don't take it personally."

"Thank you for telling me that," I said. What I meant was good luck.

"Miss Olsen, let me show you to the front door. I want to ask you some more questions."

As we passed by the door to the living room, I said, "Good night, Mrs. Fitch." I didn't get an audible response. There was some kind of grunt.

Mr. Fitch opened the front door for me to go out. He followed me out on to the sidewalk.

"Miss Olsen, are there any small things I can do to the house to make it more attractive to buyers?"

"Yes, there are. It's too late to do any major work, but the one thing you could do is have someone come in and clean out some rooms. The basement could use a thorough cleaning," I said as I thought of Mopsy or whoever. "Perhaps a cleaning company could clean and polish all the floors, too. That would help."

"Thank you, Miss Olsen. Will we see you tomorrow?"

"I will probably just come by with the sign. There's no need to bother you unless you'd like to talk to me about anything."

"Then thank you again. Good night."

I got in my car with a large sigh of relief. I didn't think I was going to pull my buns out of the fire on this one. I drove home with a feeling of accomplishment. These clients are going to be a little difficult to work with. At least Mother is, but hopefully the house will sell and produce a paycheck.

9 CHAPTER NINE

Eating bran flakes at 7:30 in the morning is one of those things you think you'll never do. When you're young, bran flakes are little brown pieces of a cardboard-like substance represented as edible by money-grubbing cereal companies. The only acceptable breakfast food is something probably sold under the name "Sugar-Soaked Crunch Flakes" or cold pizza. Somewhere along through the years, some form of nutritional wisdom takes over and things like flakes of unsweetened bran become more desirable. Not better tasting, just more sensible. It is this sensibility that indicates we are aging. There is some part of my brain that still wants cold pizza for breakfast. However, that opportunity was not present, so I was sitting at the kitchen table at 7:30 in the morning eating bran flakes. What is bran? Why is it flaked? Who decided this is good for you? The back of the box says, "Bran is the hard outer layer of cereal grains, and consists of combined aleurone and pericarp."

Ok, that tears it. I am not eating anything that contains pericarp. I wonder if that's anything like a real carp? I'd go back to cold pizza, but there wasn't any. I finished my bran flakes while reading the morning paper. After I cleaned up the dishes I thought I'd better go to the office and finish the paperwork for the Fitches' listing so Broni could put it into the system. The boys fed, I grabbed my bag and purse and went out the door. The sky was blue and the air was just right. It would probably warm up later.

"Let's get some more listings coming in, people." The voice of our illustrious leader greeted me as I walked through the office door. It was only 9:00 and he was cheer-leading as if he had an audience. I looked around to see who he was addressing and saw the two new agents cowering behind their desks in the office across the lobby from mine.

"Good morning," I said in my brightest, "I like people" voice. Dan, the office manager, looked around and rather distractedly wished me an equally good morning before wandering away. I think he was perturbed that I interrupted his pep talk.

"Hi," the new girl said somewhat timidly.

"Good morning. I'm Ophelia Olsen. Most people call me Oph. You're Nancy, is it?"

"Yes, I'm Nancy Schmidt. Have you been here long?"

Stifling the urge to say that I'd just walked in, I replied, "Yes, I'm a fixture here. I've been here for fifteen years now. It doesn't seem possible."

"This will be my first time on the floor. I'm so excited. It'll be wonderful to work with people."

"If you have any trouble, I'll be right here in my office. Just yell." I escaped to my office to avoid any more starry-eyed optimism. I don't do starry-eyed optimism well in the morning. Particularly when I had paperwork to do and other things on my mind, one of which was the remark that was made at the Fitches' last night. Mrs. Fitch had said the old fool down the street had a vacuum cleaner store and had bought a new house for a bride that wasn't going to show up. That sure sounded a lot like Mr. Bosch. Speaking of Mr. Bosch, we hadn't seen him since the morning of the dead guy on the sidewalk. If he were engaged to be married, why wouldn't he have told us? And what did Mrs. Fitch mean about the bride's not showing up? Wouldn't she already be here? Where was she showing up from? Why do I care? What would Emma Peel do? Why aren't I working on my paperwork instead of trying to put together a puzzle with a lot of missing pieces? About forty-five minutes later I finished the paperwork and took it back to Broni.

"Here you go. A new listing for you."

The large blonde head rose slowly to look at me. "I will put it in the computer in a few minutes." The head went back to looking at the paper on the desktop.

"Ok. I'm going to take a sign out to my car and I'll go put it in front of the Fitches' house a little later."

I looked down at her desk. The paper she was writing on contained three columns full of short paragraphs. I saw the name "Hubert Crowley" and "coin."

"Broni, what are you working on? Are those all clues about the murder?"

"They might be."

"What do you mean 'they might be'? It looks like it to me. Are you trying to list everything we know?"

"Maybe I am."

"Ok, what is going on?"

"I thought I could perhaps figure something out and help the police."

"Broni, we don't know that much about it. The police probably have more clues by now. How are we going to solve it when we don't have any more information than we do? All we are supposed to do is watch for foreign strangers. Speaking of whom, Crowley didn't tell us why the Latvian guy was in the village. He must have known the reason after talking to the military attaché."

Broni looked thoughtful. "I have that on my list. Detective Crowley did not tell us because it is a secret. He used the word 'operative.' The victim must have been a spy."

"A spy? What would he be spying on here? The exciting and dangerous downtown East Gilmore? There is nothing going on here. A spy would die of boredom, not blunt-force trauma."

"Maybe you do not know all that goes on here."

"And you do? What exactly is it that goes on here?"

"There might be pockets of intrigue right here in the village."

"I have to go. If you run across a pocket full of anything other than lint, call me. Bye."

As I turned to go I could swear I heard a "harrumph" behind me. Poor Broni. She thought she was going to solve the mystery. As we all know, that leads to getting your picture in the paper and being hailed as an investigative genius that the police department would want to hire. Little did she know she was no match for Emma Peel.

I went out the front door and looked around the parking lot for my baby-blue Lotus. Lo and behold, someone had substituted a small black Sentra. Good thinking. This was far more sensible. I would be too conspicuous in an exotic sports car in our little village. I drove off to place the sign in the Fitches' lawn.

It was a beautiful late spring day. The temperature was just right, the grass was a wonderful light green, the trees were starting to get the bright green of new leaves just opening up and with the car windows open, I could actually smell hyacinths. I had just turned on to Southampton Court when Mrs. Fitch's remark came back to me. She said the old fool bought a house for a bride that wasn't going to show up. I wish he would resume his schedule of stopping in the office for some of our wretched coffee, then I could question him. Subtly, of course. I would remain in my everyday garb so he wouldn't know that I am really a world-renowned spy. This would not be the time for the pointy-toes boots. The CD playing in my car was a collection of songs from various sources. The one playing at the moment was, appropriately enough, the theme from the Avengers. Emma Peel's own theme song will inspire me to solve the mystery of the missing bride. That's two mysteries in town that need solving. Emma's work is never done.

During my mental meanderings, I had driven right past the Fitches' and found myself a few houses away, in front of the house that Mr. Bosch bought. At least from what Mrs. Fitch said it sounded like Mr. Bosch. I looked over into the front yard. Mr. Bosch was looking up at a guy on a ladder who was painting a third-floor dormer. He looked toward my car, so I waved. He waved back with a puzzled look on his face. I guess he couldn't see that it was me. I had to turn around anyway, so I pulled into his driveway. He looked a little alarmed, so I rolled down my window and yelled, "Hi, Mr. Bosch." Now he looked even more alarmed, but approached the car.

"Hi. How are you? Long time no see. I was in the neighborhood putting up a sign on a house I just listed." I babbled all this rather rapidly in an attempt to assuage his obvious discomfort.

"Hi, Oph. Nice to see you." He didn't look like it was nice to see me.

"Getting some work done?"

"Just fixing it up a little. Had some peeling paint up on the trim."

"I didn't know you had moved. Have you been here long?"

"Not too long."

This seemed to be heading into uncomfortable territory. I didn't want him to start trying to apologize for not using me as his agent. Too late.

"My late wife's niece sells real estate. She is with Fred Ford. I kind of had to go to her."

"Mr. Bosch, you don't have to explain. You are free to choose any agent you wish. I assume she did a good job for you."

"Oh, yes, everything worked out fine."

"That's good," I said.

Of course, she let him pay about thirty thousand too much, but other than that she did a good job.

"I have to get going. It was good to see you again. We haven't seen too much of you lately. Is our coffee really that bad?"

He looked at the ground. "No, Oph, just been busy lately is all. I'll stop in again one of these days."

"Ok, see you." I backed out of the driveway and went down the street the way I came. I pulled up in front of the Fitches' and left the car at the curb while I took the sign out of the trunk and pounded it into the front yard. I was hoping the sound of my little handy-dandy sledge hammer wouldn't disturb the pre-prandial ruminations of Mother Fitch. I really didn't want her tottering out the front door and turning the sledge on me.

10 CHAPTER TEN

I drove back to the office just enjoying the beautiful day. The sky was a deep blue with an occasional puffy white cloud. The sunshine illuminated the spring flowers and made the world look really good. It was enough to make a body forget about the mysteries at hand. Even my parking space was still empty. Will wonders never cease?

I opened the front door to hear the new girl, Nancy, telling a customer on the phone that a listing was probably over-priced. I stood there in amazement. This is her first time answering phones and she is an expert already?

I put my bag down in my office and went back out to the front desk.

"Nancy, can I talk to you for a minute?"

"Oh, yes, Oph, of course."

I walked around to the front of the desk and looked into Nancy's eyes. I was trying to see if there was anything behind them. She moved back a little. I may have looked threatening.

"Nancy, did you just tell a complete stranger that one of our listings was overpriced?"

"Uh, I guess I did. But I was just agreeing with him."

"He said he thought it was overpriced? And your opinion is that it is overpriced?"

"I thought it must be if he thought so."

"Nancy, you are the real estate agent. He is not. His opinion is based on hot air. Yours should be based on the fact that an agent with far more experience than you has priced that house. Now, it may not be exactly right, but I guarantee you some thought and research went into that price, not just hot air. When you tell the public that our listings are overpriced, you are telling them that we are idiots. It may be overpriced, but there may be a reason for it. If someone tells you that again, just ask in your sweetest voice if they would like to see the house. Ok?"

She looked like a bunny that had just been terrorized by a crow. I was just trying to give her a few facts, not scare her to death. I guess I had forgotten what it was like to be new.

She finally spoke. "I'm sorry. I will know better next time."

"That's ok, Nancy. That's how you learn. Just relax. Remember that we price the houses as best we can. No one can predict with 100% accuracy how much any house will sell for. It's the market that sets the price. It's whatever a buyer is willing to pay. Anyway, you'll do fine."

I walked down the hallway to see how Broni was coming with her clues.

"As I live and breathe, if it isn't Miss Marple solving another crime for the village constabulary," I said as I walked through her door.

Broni looked up from her desk. She did not appear to be amused by my witty greeting. She put her head back down and stared at the piece of paper with the clues on it.

"Hey, Broni, has Mr. Bosch been in?"

"No, I have not seen him," she muttered.

"Well, I found out something interesting. When I was at Southampton getting that listing last night, one of the owners mentioned an old fool down the street that paid too much for a house for his new bride. She also said he owned a vacuum cleaner store."

Broni looked up. "Was he talking about Mr. Bosch?"

"Well, it's a she, a very old she, and I wasn't sure at the time. So, today when I took the yard sign over there I went down the street a little further and saw Mr. Bosch out in front of the house. He was having some painting done."

"Did you talk to him?"

"Just for a minute. I had to pull in his driveway to turn around and I told him I didn't know he had moved. He said he hadn't been there long. He seemed uncomfortable and said he had to use his late wife's niece as his agent. That may have been the reason. Maybe he thought I'd be hurt or insulted that he hadn't used one of us, since he stops in here every day. Or used to, anyway. I told him we hadn't seen him in a while and asked if our coffee was really that bad. He just said he had been busy. So, my hunch was right. It was Mr. Bosch that bought the house."

"What about the bride?"

"I certainly didn't ask him. Oh, also the old lady said the bride would never show up."

At that Broni looked up. "Never show up? What does she mean by that?"

"That's another mystery."

The idea of another mystery to solve got Broni out of her mood in short order.

"Maybe we should go visit Mr. Bosch if he won't come here," she said.

"What are going to say to him? We can't just barge into the store and ask how the bride got lost."

"Maybe I need new bags for my vacuum cleaner."

"So we both go traipsing into his store and while we are picking out bags, just happen to ask if he has thought about getting married again? How subtle is that?"

"No, it has to be much cleverer. I will think about this."

"Ok, you do that. Meanwhile, I am on the phones from noon to three, so I'll be up at the front desk awaiting your thoughts."

I think she gave me a dirty look as I turned and walked down the hall.

The phones weren't ringing that afternoon, so I sat there wondering about Mr. Bosch. All of a sudden this seemed more interesting than the dead-guy mystery. The down side is that this one was too much of a domestic problem and not the kind of thing that Emma Peel would get involved in. I guess it was of some interest because we knew Mr. Bosch, but now that Bert Crowley had told us there was classified information involved, the dead guy became more appropriate for Emma Peel. Thinking back, it was Broni who called it classified. I think the detective said confidential. Close enough. Obviously this was work worthy of Emma Peel's successor.

Three o'clock came and the next duty agent took over. I wandered back to Broni's office wondering what we should be doing next. It also occurred to me that we probably shouldn't be doing anything. Detective Crowley said to just keep our eyes and ears open. Actually he was more interested in Broni's eyes and ears because of the Latvian connection. I was just a set of auxiliary visual and auditory body parts, most of which he didn't appear to be interested in.

"So, how are the clues coming? Have you seen or heard anything about strangers of the Latvian persuasion in town?"

"No, not yet. I am going to my friend Aija's house for dinner tonight and I have asked her for you to come also."

Shivers ran through my stomach. Is Aija's cooking anything like Broni's? My query was answered by Broni.

"She likes to try different recipes. She is a very good cook."

"Uh, thanks. I have to check and see if there is anything on my calendar tonight."

"Please come, Oph. I want you to be there in case anything

sounds suspicious to you that I might miss."

The desire to be present if this Aija reveals any interesting information was far stronger than my possibly unfounded dread of her cooking.

"Ok. I'll go. I don't think I have anything going on tonight. Where does she live?"

"Just come to my house. We can walk there together. It is only a few blocks."

"What time?"

"Come about 5:30. She will serve dinner at 6 o'clock."

"I'll be there. See you later."

I went down the hallway and out the front door. I drove home thinking about tonight. That would be really exciting if Broni's friend had some news about strangers in town. This would certainly make Detective Crowley think twice about my sleuthing abilities. Never mind that it was actually Broni's connection that got the information. Perhaps she would let me tell him about it and he would not only recognize me as a crack detective, but as a possible resource in future cases. This would, of course, ultimately lead to an international reputation as the probable successor to Emma Peel.

I pulled into the garage after watching my door rise, imaginary bushes and all. I really need to prune the hedges and find a large container of epoxy.

I pulled into Broni's driveway about 5:25. She must have been watching for me because the door opened before I rang the bell.

"Hello, Oph. Come in." She swung the door back and I went in to her living room.

"Oh, Broni, you've got a new couch! When did you get that?"

"It was on sale at the Ton-Ton home store. Do you like it?"

I did like it. I had been looking for one like that for a long time. My couch was about forty-five years old and sadly in need of some work.

"Do they have any more like that?"

"No, Oph, it was the last one."

Just my luck. The foam rubber inside my couch cushions disintegrated due to old age and was falling out onto the carpet in what looked like little piles of cornmeal. My living room floor looked like a grain mill.

"Oh, well. I'll just have to keep looking. I like that style. It looks almost Victorian."

"I like it because it is large. I can lie down on it without bumping my head."

She was right. That couch had to be seven feet long.

"I will get my coat. It is time to go."

Broni got her coat out of the closet in the hall and locked the front door.

"Let's go out the back door. I can lock it from the outside."

"Can't you lock the front door?"

"Only from the inside. There is no key."

I followed her out the back door onto her little porch. She carefully locked her door and we set out to walk the two blocks to Aija's house.

"Is Aija married?"

"No. She was, but her husband was not a good man. He left her with the two babies."

"How long ago was this?"

"Two years ago. One baby was newborn and the other was one and a half years."

"Where did he go?"

"I don't know. He was involved with some bad people and may have gone back to Latvia."

"How does Aija support herself? Does she work?"

"Yes, she is a waitress at the little coffee shop on Main Street just two blocks down from the office."

"Oh, I don't think I've ever been in there."

"Sometimes I go there to get coffee and see Aija."

"Oh. You told me you had a friend that worked there. I guess I never knew her name."

We were just approaching Aija's porch as I finished my interrogation of Broni. She tromped up the steps and knocked on the door of the little bungalow. It looked like Broni's house, except a little smaller. It seemed to be equally as well-kept.

The front door opened and a smaller version of Broni stood there. Aija was very thin with a drawn face that belied her age. She couldn't have been more than thirty, but looked about fifty. Her dark blonde hair was drawn back in a severe bun and she wore no makeup.

"Come in, please," she said quietly.

Broni hugged her rather gently and I shook her hand.

"Hello, Aija. Thank you for having me come here tonight."

I had listened very carefully to Broni's pronunciation of her name and hoped I had gotten it right.

"Oh, I am so happy to have you. Please sit down."

I looked around at the furniture. There was a threadbare couch and two overstuffed armchairs. At least they used to be overstuffed. It appeared that the stuffing was on its way out. Aija had contained it by pinning small towels to the arms. It looked rather homey. Sitting on the couch were two small blonde girls that looked like miniature Aijas. They looked up at us and broke into grins when they saw Broni. They hopped off the couch together and ran to her, hugging her legs. She bent down and scooped them up in her arms. She kissed both of them on their little red cheeks. She then proceeded to speak to them in what was to me a totally unintelligible manner. I presumed it was Latvian.

Aija was beaming at them. It was a revelation to me to see Broni in this light. I had never seen her with little kids before. She would have been a good mother. She carried them to the couch and gently set them down. Then she sat between them and picked up the book they had been reading. The three of them looked intently at the pictures.

"Please, Miss Olsen, sit down," Aija said, pointing at one of the armchairs. I sat. She sat in the other one.

Wonderful smells were wafting through the archway from the kitchen. It didn't smell like Broni's cooking. Aija said she had to check on something and went into the kitchen. I watched Broni with the little girls. She was reading out of the book to them. They were giggling quietly. Either it was a funny book, or she was making stuff up. I certainly couldn't tell the difference.

"Dinner is almost ready. I hope you are hungry?" Aija said as she came back into the room.

"Yes, I am and it smells delicious."

Broni gave me a funny look. I had begged off dinner at her house several times with various excuses involving food allergies. Methinks my deception may have caught up with me. I had better refuse at least one food type on the basis of an allergy.

Aija looked at the girls. "Go and wash your hands, please."

They hopped off the couch and ran off to the bathroom.

"Come, Miss Olsen, into the kitchen and sit down at the table."

"Aija, please call me Oph or even Ophelia. You don't have to call me Miss Olsen."

She smiled and nodded. I sat down in a well-worn wooden chair at the kitchen table. Broni sat to my left on the end. I noticed that the two chairs on the opposite side had old phone books stacked on them. As the two girls ran into the kitchen, their mother lifted each one up and set them down on their respective phone books.

I looked at Broni and said quietly, "Now I know why you took the old phone books from the office."

She just smiled.

Aija picked up a platter and handed it to me. "Please help yourself, Oph." I was glad she stopped calling me Miss Olsen, even if she did pronounce my name more like "Oof."

I took a piece of whatever was on the plate. She then proceeded to pass a bowl of potatoes and a bowl of green beans. After taking some of each and passing them on to Broni, I decided to investigate the thing I took off the platter. I cut a little piece and put it in my mouth. I was astounded. It was the most delicious piece of chicken I had ever tasted.

"Aija, this is very good. I have never had such good chicken. What did you put on it?"

Right away I knew something was up. Broni and Aija looked at each other and smiled. In fact Broni was having a hard time containing herself. I would gladly have kicked her in the kneecap, but being a guest in someone's home kind of puts a damper on that. I just sat there chewing and wondering when they were going to tell me what I was eating. I ran through several possibilities in my head. It was too wide for rattlesnake. It was too rectangular for squid.

"Oof, I am sorry, I should have told you. It is turtle. The meat is very like chicken and I put some spices on it and cooked it for a long time. You like it, yes?"

As much as the idea of eating a large hard-shelled amphibian repelled me, it was good. It had a nice mild flavor and the spices just set it off.

"I have to admit, I have never eaten turtle before, but it is quite good." At that I looked at Broni to prove to her that I was an adventurer and could handle meat substances other than cow or chicken. She looked a little surprised, but smiled.

The two little girls were eating tiny squares of turtle that their mother had cut up and put on their plates.

I was wondering how Aija could afford this. I would think turtle would fall under the category of exotic meat and might be expensive.

"Where do you get turtle meat? Does the Stop and Shop here have it?" I couldn't imagine that they did. I had only been in there once and it barely had hamburger, say nothing about turtle.

Aija looked a little uncomfortable. I hoped I hadn't said something wrong.

Broni looked up and said, "Aija's brother brought it to her. He lives about fifteen miles out into the country. He has a pond on his land."

Oh, I got it, she couldn't afford anything else. Now to extract my foot from my mouth gracefully.

"Oh, how nice. I didn't know you had a brother here. Do you see him often?"

"Yes, quite often. He brings us fresh vegetables from his garden and some fish and turtles from his pond."

"He must be a very nice man. How lucky you are to have him." I was really going to town on the extraction process.

We ate on until our plates were empty. Aija brought out a beautiful pie.

"My brother brought us some cherries from his freezer. He picked them off his trees last summer." She started to cut small wedges and place them on little plates on the table.

"Aija, please make mine a very small piece. I am quite full." It was the truth. I had eaten a large turtle steak and vegetables and didn't need much more.

As good as all the food was, while I ate my pie, I wondered when we might be able to ask a few questions and see what Aija might know about the comings and goings of any possible suspects in the murder case.

We all finished, including the little girls. Aija cleared the table with some help from Broni and me. She put the food in the refrigerator and the dishes in the dishpan.

She asked us to go back into the living room. Broni and I sat in the armchairs and Aija sat on the couch holding her two little ones. They started nodding off.

"It looks like a couple of us are sleepy," I said, almost starting to yawn myself.

"I will put them to bed. Please be comfortable and I will be back in a few minutes."

Aija picked up the younger girl and took the hand of the other and they went through a hallway at the end of the living room.

"Broni, when she comes back can we ask her about any strangers she may have seen?"

Broni gave me her best TV investigator look and proceeded to explain.

"Yes, but we must be very careful. I do not want to ask obvious questions, because we do not want to make her suspicious about why we are asking. If she knows why we are asking, she may get curious and put herself in danger. We cannot take that chance. It has to be a casual conversation."

I couldn't argue with that. Broni was right. We could not let Aija get involved in this. She is the sole support of those two little girls.

"Who watches the girls while she is at work?"

"There is an aunt who lives close by. She keeps them at her house."

"The aunt doesn't work?"

"Yes, but at night. She works in the auto factory over by the river."

"And watches two little kids during the day?"

"Yes, she is very busy."

And very tired, I could imagine. These women worked extremely hard just to survive. It made me feel guilty about my complaints.

After a few minutes Aija came back into the living room.

"They are both asleep," she said.

"They are very cute and well-behaved, Aija," I said.

"Thank you. They are the light in my life."

"And you are theirs, I'm sure. And they seem to like Broni well enough, too."

"They love Bronislawa. She is like the grandmother to them."

I chuckled to myself at the look on Broni's face. I think she wanted to be thought of more like an aunt than a grandmother.

"Broni is certainly the grandmotherly type, alright." I couldn't resist.

Broni shot me a rather disgruntled look and said to Aija, "Is there any news in the neighborhood?"

Aija looked down at her hands. "I have heard that Mikelis has been seen."

Broni looked alarmed. "When was that? Did he come here?"

Aija waved her arms and shook her head. "No, no, he did not come here. For that I thank the Good Lord. Aunt Laima heard this through her brother-in-law."

I was looking at Broni for an explanation of who this Mikelis was.

"Mikelis is Aija's former husband. I told you about him."

"Oh, right, I remember." He was the bad one that may have gone back to the old country.

Broni turned to Aija. "Does she know what he was doing here?"

"No, only that he was with another man."

"Is he still here?" I ventured to ask.

"I am not sure. They were only seen once."

"Is your aunt sure it was Mikelis?" I asked. They both turned and looked at me.

Broni said, "Mikelis cannot be mistaken. He lost a hand in an accident and he is very handsome."

Ok, so she may be right. How many one-handed handsome guys could there be? I can't even locate a two-handed handsome guy.

I was hoping Broni would ask some more questions. I didn't know what to ask because I didn't know Mikelis' history of evil doings. She didn't disappoint me.

"Aija, do you have any ideas of what he was doing here?"

"No, I only know that when he left, he said he didn't want to stay here anymore, that he was going to make a lot of money back in our home land."

"I thought people came here to get a new start and be able to make more money?" I asked, based on a major generalization. It didn't make sense to me that going home to a little Latvian village could be profitable.

Broni spoke. "That is right for most people, Oph. Mikelis must have had something in mind that he thought would make money."

Aija spoke, slowly at first. "It probably was something that was not legal. Mikelis changed after we came here. He talked about money all the time. He saw people here who had big cars and big houses and it changed him. He didn't care about the babies anymore." By the time she finished she was sobbing into her apron.

"Aija, I'm sorry for what you've been through. There are a lot of people here that do that, too. They can't be happy with what they have," I said, trying to make her feel better, which was a lost cause at this point. This Mikelis twerp must be a real winner to run out on a wife and two little girls.

"Mikelis will come to no good if he continues to think this way. You are better off without him, Aija. You are teaching the girls right and wrong. If he were here they would learn to be criminals," Broni said with a disgusted look.

Aija sat up and wiped her eyes. "Thank you. I know you are right. Oof, I am sorry. I am not being a very good hostess."

"Aija, you are being a perfectly good hostess. I am just sorry that your husband disappointed you so."

"It is getting late. I have to go to work early and so does Aija. Oph, we should go," Broni said as she lumbered up out of her chair.

I gracefully arose from mine and walked to the couch. Aija stood up. I took her hands and said. "Thank you for a lovely dinner. It was a great pleasure to meet you and the children. Do your girls like cats?"

Aija smiled. "Yes, they love them."

"Good. Then you will have to bring them to my house. We will all have dinner and the girls can meet George and Ira. You too, Broni."

We all went to the front door. Aija opened it. Broni and I stepped out onto the little porch and went down the steps. From the sidewalk we both waved and bid goodnight to Aija.

We started walking toward Broni's house. I was the first to speak. "What was that business with Mikelis all about?"

"I am not sure. It is very odd that he was back here. It is also odd that he did not try to contact Aija or the children. When they first got married he was a nice young man. At least I think he was or she wouldn't have married him. Shortly after that they came over here, about five years ago, I think. I met them then, although I remember Aija's mother as a child in Latvia. She is about my age. Before too long, Mikelis was talking about other people's things."

"That's what Aija said. What did Mikelis do for a living?"

"He worked at the iron foundry. The one that the Fitches started."

"Well, it was actually Mrs. Fitch's father, old Oliver Abernethy. Hence the name Abernethy Iron. Anyway, Is that where Mikelis lost his hand?"

"Yes, there was an accident somewhere in the foundry."

"So, you said he left about two years ago. Has he been seen here since?"

"No, as far as I know this is the first time."

"So, the big question is: Does he have anything to do with the dead guy?"

We had just reached Broni's side door. I fished my keys out of my purse. Broni was standing there looking very thoughtful.

"Oph, why would Mikelis have any connection to the dead guy?"

"Why not? Think about what we know. First of all, Detective Crowley said to watch out for any strangers in town, probably Latvian nationals. Aija said Mikelis told her he was going home to make a lot of money. He was seen here with another man, obviously a stranger, since the aunt didn't know him. Murders quite often coincide with people being involved in something that would make a lot of money, particularly something illegal. Both you and Aija said Mikelis was probably involved in something illegal. See, it all adds up. We can practically claim our reward for solving the crime."

Broni's large head was pointed up at the sky, looking at the stars. I presumed she was channeling an inhabitant of another galaxy and we would have an important pronouncement any moment. Finally she spoke.

"What evidence do we have to connect Mikelis to the murder? He is just a two-bit criminal that came back."

"Aha! Why did he come back? Why didn't he just stay home and make money? He didn't contact Aija or the kids, so that isn't it. He may just be here as part of his nefarious get-rich-quick scheme. Something may have gone wrong and the murder became necessary. Maybe he didn't do it; maybe the other guy did. What makes it unlikely that he is a part of this?"

Broni walked around in circles for a minute, kind of like a wolf making a place to lie down. She looked back up at the stars for more cosmic inspiration.

"Oph, you may be right. What if he came here as part of his money-making plan and something went wrong?"

Is there an echo in here? Didn't I just say the same thing?

"Exactly, Broni. He is mixed up in this somehow. Think about it. I have to go home and go to bed."

I got in my car and yelled out the window. "Thanks for taking me along tonight. I'll see you in the morning."

I drove home with all kinds of thoughts whirling around in my head. Emma Peel would have figured this all out by now, I'm sure. Of course that's because she only had 26 minutes in each episode. Fortunately, I have longer than that. I'm going to need it.

11 CHAPTER ELEVEN

I woke up to the familiar sounds of chirping. At my house, chirping in the morning did not come from the cheerful little birdies outside my window, but from the hungry pussycats on the bed. Trying to blink the grogginess out of my eyes wasn't working, so I rolled off the mattress and wandered into the bathroom, where I proceeded to splash prodigious amounts of cold water on my face. It started to have the desired effect after a few moments but was taking longer than usual because I had not slept well. I spent much of the night, or so it seemed, pondering the circumstances surrounding Mikelis' return to East Gilmore.

I had not come up with any good theories. There was still too much information missing. We still did not know the dead guy's mission here. If we knew what he was investigating, this might make more sense.

The three of us ate breakfast in relative silence. I wanted to go out and work in the yard this morning. I didn't have to be at the office until later, so this would be a good chance to weed some of the flower beds.

The sun was getting quite warm by the time I quit pulling weeds. I probably pulled a few flowers too, but they all looked alike in the spring. I kicked off my muddy shoes outside the back door and went in the house. I passed by the answering machine on my way upstairs. It was beeping at me. There were two messages. I listened to the first one. It was from Broni. She wondered when I would be coming in to the office, because she had to talk to me. The second one was also from Broni with the same message. I proceeded upstairs to bathe and put on my office clothes. I finished up by combing my hair and applying just a hint of makeup to enhance my natural beauty. Ok, so I got that last bit off a TV commercial. It made me feel better. I pulled into the parking lot, taking note of the other cars. There was Broni's GiantMobile, Don's tiny little rattletrap ("But it gets good mileage") and a gray car I didn't recognize. Maybe it belonged to a customer. I soon found out who the other car belonged to. It was an unmarked police car and in the office stood Detective Crowley.

"Good morning Detective," I chirruped in my most Emma Peel-like voice. I did everything but the English accent. "How is your investigation going?" I have to admit, I may have batted my eyes just a teensy.

"It's coming along slowly. I just stopped in to see if you or Ms. Z had run across anything yet."

"Let's go back to Broni's office and see if she knows anything." I wanted to be there when we both told him about Mikelis and the stranger.

"Broni, Detective Crowley is here to see if we know anything yet." She was staring intently at Crowley.

"Hello, Detective Crowley. I am afraid I haven't heard anything yet from any of my contacts."

I stared at her in disbelief.

"Uh, Broni, what about ..." I only got that much out of my mouth before Broni shot me the freezing stare. "Checking with your friend today. Maybe that would be good."

She let up a little on the intensity and turned back to the detective. In her sweetest voice, she said, "Yes, that's a good idea. I will check with my friend today and call you if there is any news."

The detective was a little more astute than we thought. He looked at Broni, then at me. I, of course, let him have it with my most devastatingly gorgeous smile. For some reason he seemed to be unaffected by it. He still was looking at us as though we had something to hide.

"Ladies, I hope you will let me know immediately when you have any news that might be of interest to me. It could be very important to this case."

"Yes, Detective. As soon as we have anything useful to you we will call."

"Please do. Good afternoon, ladies."

"Good-bye, Detective Crowley," we both said at the same time.

He turned and looked at us again. It's just my hunch that he was starting to get suspicious.

After we heard him go out the front door, I turned to Broni and hissed loudly, "What are you doing? Are you out of your mind? Why didn't you tell him about Mikelis and the stranger?"

She sat down at her desk and then proceeded to speak to me in her TV crime-fighter voice.

"Because Aija still thinks Mikelis will become his old self again and come back to her. I don't want to turn him in yet until we find out why he is here. If it is just to reconcile with his family, I don't want to hurt their chances."

"Broni, you are nuts. Aija herself said that he had turned into a rotten apple. Why would you think he would change back again?"

"I just want to check a little more before we tell the police that he might be a suspect."

"MIGHT BE? How about IS? He hasn't made any contact with Aija. I think this is crazy. What if he gets away?"

"Please, Oph, let it be this way for just a short time," she said.

"Ok, but we can't waste too much time. How are you going to find out what he's doing?"

"We will go on a stakeout." She beamed from ear to ear. "Oph, why do you put your head down in your hands? Do you not think this is a good idea?"

"Yes, I do not think this is a good idea. What if the bad guys see us first? Detective Crowley said we were not to get anywhere near anybody that might be a bad guy. They get the name 'bad guy' for a reason and it isn't showing up late for Bible study. Remember that?"

"I remember, but we are not going to go near them. We will just park the car and hide and use the digital camera to zoom in on them."

"Oh, good. And when the flash goes off, we'll just hope they blink and don't notice it."

"Oph, you are being so difficult. We will not take pictures with a flash. We will just use the zoom lens to see them, and maybe take a picture without the flash if we see anything interesting. We have to find out what Mikelis is doing here."

"Why don't we just ask Aunt What's-her-name, the one who saw him."

"Because she just saw him, she didn't observe his movements or talk to him. She doesn't know any more than we do."

"I'll bet she does, I'll bet she knows enough not to go gallivanting off on some wild goose chase that could put her life in danger."

"You don't know that your life will be in danger and we are not chasing wild gooses. Why do you say we are chasing wild gooses?"

"It's just an old expression. When will this take place?"

"Tomorrow night. It will be just a quarter moon."

"And exactly where is it that you propose to park, since we don't know the subject's whereabouts?"

"I will find out where Aunt Laima saw him and we will start from there. See? It is simple."

"The only thing here that is simple is me, if I go along with this. I just don't think it is going to work and it sounds dangerous."

"Then I will go alone." She got up from her desk, pulled open the top drawer of the filing cabinet and started stuffing folders in it.

Muttering to myself, I went back to my office.

"Oph, call on line one," Nancy, the new agent yelled out.

"Hello, this is Ophelia Olsen."

"Miss Olsen, this is Alfred Fitch. I have a problem. The girl from your office called here to schedule a showing appointment for tomorrow afternoon. I have to take Mother to a doctor's appointment about the same time. Is it possible for you to come stay at the house to let in the agent and his client?"

"Of course, Mr. Fitch. I will be happy to. I'll let them in and then lock up when they are done. We don't want to turn down any showings."

"No, we don't. We would like to sell the house as fast as possible. What have the people who have seen the house been saying about it?"

"I've gotten various comments. I have them summarized for you. Why don't I come a few minutes early tomorrow and we can go over them before you have to leave for the doctor."

"That would be fine, Miss Olsen. The appointment is for 1:30."

"Very good, Mr. Fitch, I'll see you a little before one. Goodbye."

"Goodbye, Miss Olsen."

I hung up the phone. I will have to go more than a few

minutes early. I had a whole list of opinions about the house and he wasn't going to like most of them.

Getting back to the previous problem, I can't let Broni go alone tomorrow night. It would be very cowardly of me and suicidal for her. Emma Peel would never let a friend go unsupported into the face of peril. On the other hand, I am not really Emma Peel so what do I care?

The answer is obvious. I can't let Broni go alone. Perhaps I can watch some reruns of the Avengers to prepare for a stakeout. I know that Emma and John always had champagne with them. I'm not sure that would work for us. I would probably fall asleep.

I sat at my desk for a few more minutes. I was surprised that Broni hadn't come to ask if I were really serious about letting her go alone. Maybe she should stew for a little while longer.

I got busy summarizing the comments on the showings of the Fitch house. I made a list categorizing the areas of complaint. I'll explain all this to them tomorrow. I hope Mother Fitch is busy applying lime dust and nitrates to her face or whatever she uses for a preservative, when I first get there. That way I can just talk to Alfred. Oh, well. I'll deal with that tomorrow. Meanwhile, it's twenty minutes since I left Broni's office. I guess I'd better make the first move. I marched down the hall to the back office.

"Ok, have you come to your senses yet?" I said to Broni's back as she stood filing.

Silence. I walked around so I could see the side of her face. It looked like it had been chiseled out of stone. Her eyes never wavered from the files.

"Broni, do you really think this stakeout is going to do any good?"

More silence. I am coming to the conclusion my continued attempts to talk her out of this are failing. I should know better than to try to change her mind when the stone-faced visage is in place.

"Alright, you win. What time should I be at your house?"

She turned around with a smile. Amazing how fast it can change.

"It gets dark about 7:30. Come then."

"What should I bring? I don't have any police equipment. I'm fresh out of handcuffs and those little cards that have the Miranda thing on them."

"Do you have a flashlight? And bring your camera."

"Ok. I'm going home now. It is time for me to sit quietly and ponder my sanity."

Broni walked over and stood right in front of me. Now what have I done?

"Thank you, Oph. I promise we will be very careful and just see what we can see. And also we will leave if anything dangerous happens."

"You got that one right. We will leave very fast if anything dangerous happens. I'm also fresh out of pointy-toed boots."

I walked out of her office leaving her thinking about that one.

I went home and walked into the living room, relieved to be in a quiet place, devoid of humanity. I just wanted to let my mind wander and not focus on anything. Particularly on trying to solve a mystery. I sat down in my chair and stared aimlessly at the floor. The rug was an Oriental design with bright flowers and abstract figures of reds and blues. Today the rug seemed to have a gray haze over it. I must be letting this mystery get to me. I'm overworked or maybe it's cataracts. I had better call the eye doctor. Now to think about where the phone book might be. I was still staring at the rug when I began to see a pattern in the gray haze. It almost looked like little fibers. I got down closer to the floor and discovered the rug was covered with a fine mat of cat hair.

At this point I decided that I had been neglecting some simple household chores long enough and vacuuming the house would be a desirable thing to accomplish. Maybe just the downstairs. I don't want to get compulsive about this cleanliness business.

I went into the den and opened the closet door to extract the vacuum cleaner and its hoses and nozzles. The bag was full so I reached for a new one, only to discover that I had none. Oh, woe is me. This will have to be postponed another day or two, until I have time to visit Mr. Bosch and buy some new bags. Any maybe ask a couple of questions.

12 CHAPTER TWELVE

Most days pass quietly around the village. Or at least they used to back in the olden days before the dead guy showed up. We were a happy little collection of stores, shops, offices and the like. Nobody had to worry what to wear on a stakeout or if whatever you wore might come in contact with a blunt object wielded by a group of evildoers known colloquially as "bad guys." We just went about our business totally insulated from the world of crime and wrong-doing. Now, don't get me wrong, we had our share of petty stuff. Things like taking back a soda pop bottle that didn't belong to you and keeping the nickel, not giving the Avon lady back her catalog when she specifically asked you to, unpaid overdue book fines galore, and even one case of bona fide wife-swapping. I think that last one got rectified as soon as the swappers realized that the swappees were worse than the originals.

My point is that this latest problem, specifically that of a dead guy on the sidewalk, followed by the Latvian Consulate identifying him as one of their operatives and the criminals that caused him to be deceased, is quite a bit beyond the comprehension of our populace and by extension, our police department. Not that the police personnel are lacking in intelligence, just practice. Whatever skills they have are probably a little rusty.

This is what I was thinking as I pulled into the parking lot the next afternoon. I had about forty-five minutes before I had to leave to babysit the Fitch house.

"Broni, are you back there?" I yelled as I came through the front door. Don, the office manager, peeked out of his office.

"Oph, please don't yell in here. There are people on the telephone conducting business."

I glanced at the nearest telephone as I walked down the hall. None of the lines were lit up and the front desk duty agent was filing her nails.

"Sorry, Don, I can certainly see the new people are just prospecting up a storm on those telephones." He smiled and went back in his office. Another good job done.

"Broni. I have a flashlight and my camera is in my car. Whose car are we taking tonight?"

"Yours, Oph. It is small and black and mine is large. Yours will be much less conspicuous."

"Oh, good, that way the nefarious nightcrawlers will have my license number."

"Ophelia. You attitude is very negative. We must keep the energy with us. We have to have the correct view of this mission."

Mission? Heaven help us.

"Ok, Sherlock. I'll talk to you later. I have to go over to the Fitch house for a showing."

I still had about a half-hour before I had to appear. I remembered the vacuum cleaner bags and decided to pay Mr. Bosch a visit. Maybe I can kill two birds with one stone.

His store was only two blocks down the street, so I walked. As I neared the front door of the vacuum cleaner store I noticed the big display in his window. It was a vacuum cleaner with a funny-looking funnel attachment holding up a bowling ball. The sign indicated that this feat could only be performed with a very strong machine typified by the particular brand advertised. This may be fine for some people, but all I really want is for my cleaner to pick up cat hair, some dust and maybe little bits of paper off the floor. If I need my bowling ball elevated for any reason, I will probably do it manually. To each his own.

As I opened the front door, the little bell hanging over it tinkled my presence. Mr. Bosch came out of the back room and looked surprised to see me.

"Hello, Ophelia. Nice to see you again. What can I do for you?"

"Well, Mr. Bosch, yesterday I was stricken with the unaccustomed urge to vacuum my carpet. It seems that cat hair has reached the level where it is obscuring my view of the brightly colored designs. Alas, when I went to my closet to retrieve a new bag for the cleaner, I found that I had none. That is the reason for my visit."

And to see what else I can find out.

"What kind of cleaner do you have, Oph?"

"I think it is a Whirling Dervish Number Nine, if I'm not mistaken."

"I think you're right. I remember the last time you came in. That isn't a very common machine and you are the only one who ever asked for bags for one."

"I bought the cleaner from you a few years ago, remember? It was a used one."

"Oh, that's right. It had been sitting around here for a while. Those are very good and quite expensive when they're new. Do you still like it?"

"Yes, I do. It seems to have a lot of suction and the brush keeps going no matter what size dust ball it runs into. Around my house they can get pretty big."

Mr. Bosch laughed and put the bags into a shopping bag and handed it to me.

"How much are they?" I asked, getting out my wallet.

"Six dollars and forty-eight cents, including tax." He rang up the sale on the cash register.

I handed him a ten-dollar bill. "Did you get the painting done on your new house?"

He looked up as he handed me back my change. "Yes, it's all done. Oph, I would have rather had you for that house than my late wife's niece, but I felt I had to use her."

"Mr. Bosch. You don't have to apologize. You already told me about your wife's niece that day I turned around in your driveway. It's perfectly alright. Now tell me about your house. Are you getting settled?"

"Oh, somewhat. I still have a ways to go. I didn't keep much of my old furniture. I needed to get new stuff anyway and this house is bigger than my old one. I'll need more things."

"So you are upsizing. A lot of people I know are trying to downsize a little later in life."

There, I'd stuck my foot in my mouth. I hoped it had the desired effect.

"Well, I'm thinking that maybe if I ever get married again, I would like a nicer house."

"Why, Mr. Bosch, I didn't know you cared. I am single now, and I love big houses." I laughed as I said it. Fortunately, he laughed, too.

"Oph, I would be honored, but I am engaged."

"You are? Congratulations! Why didn't you say anything?"

"Well, the arrangements have just recently been completed."

"Where is she? Are you going to let us meet her? Is she from here?"

"No, she's not from here. She will be arriving in another two weeks or so and I wanted to keep it a secret and surprise everybody, so I am not going to say any more."

"Oh, come on. You can't keep us in suspense. Wait 'til I tell Broni. She'll be surprised. When is the wedding?"

"I don't know just yet. She needs to get here before we plan anything."

"Where is she coming from?"

"Ophelia, I told you I'm not going to say anything more just now." He picked up my vacuum bags and handed them to me as he hustled me out the door.

"Alright. I'll let you off the hook for now. You had better stop in and have coffee soon, though, and tell us some more."

"Ok, Oph. I'll see you." He turned and went back into his shop.

I stood there for a moment, wondering about what I had just heard. So, there was a bride. Mr. Bosch said she would be here in a couple of weeks. Mrs. Fitch had said the bride would never arrive. Curious.

I walked back to the parking lot and got in my car. I had about ten minutes to get to the Fitch house.

I pulled up in front of the big house on Southampton Court with about three minutes to spare. I wanted to talk to Mr. Fitch before he took Mother to the doctor.

I reached out to ring the bell just as the door opened.

"Hello, Miss Olsen, right on time. Please come in." Mr. Fitch stood aside as I entered the foyer.

"Good afternoon, Mr. Fitch. How are you?"

"Very well, thank you. Let's go into the library. I believe you have something to show me while I wait for Mother."

I followed Alfred across the foyer and the living room, through a beautiful door in an entire wall of oak linenfold paneling. The library was equally as spectacular. This room was walnut. About twenty-four feet long by fifteen feet wide, the ratio of the Golden Rectangle. Bookcases covered three walls. The fourth wall was windows that looked out on the rear gardens. A huge Oriental rug covered the center of the room. It had a beige background with a large maroon and dark blue medallion in the center. And no cat fur. Must be they

116

vacuumed. Well, probably not either one of them. Most likely a cleaning lady or ladies.

Mr. Fitch gestured to a dark red leather club chair. "Please have a seat, Miss Olsen."

"Thank you, Mr. Fitch." He sat down in a chair opposite mine. "I have gathered some of the comments from the agents who have shown your home. We have had quite a few showings for the time that the house has been on the market. Most of the comments follow the same pattern. The clients loved the space, the layout, the woodwork and the gardens, but were discouraged by the amount of work that would have to be done to bring the house up to the needs of their lifestyles."

I sat silently after this, wondering what his response would be.

"Miss Olsen, I understand perfectly. I know that younger people, particularly ones with families, will want more modern appurtenances. Neither Mother or I put much of a strain upon the electrical system."

I could only presume that after Mother's complaint of constipation during my last visit, that they didn't put much of a strain on the plumbing either.

"My suggestion would be to offer a little bit of an incentive. Perhaps a few thousand dollars in the form of an allowance to be given to the purchaser at closing to help cover the cost of a new electrical system or a new boiler. It might help convince someone to look at the good points of the house and realize that the rest can be fixed."

Alfred looked thoughtful. "Miss Olsen, I can understand the wisdom of your suggestion. I will need to convince Mother that it is a good one. She remembers when the household mechanical systems were new and has difficulty grasping the idea that they have aged, just as she has."

"Aged, my ass, Alfred. They are decrepit just like I am and I do too understand." The voice preceded the appearance by a split second. Mother Fitch came through the library door accompanied by the tap of the walker. "Miss Olsen, do whatever you have to do to sell this place. I have decided it is time to move on. Alfred, stop giving her such a hard time."

"Did you hear my suggestion, Mrs. Fitch?" I went straight for the decision maker. "I think the idea of a financial incentive to be used for plumbing or electrical or heating work might help generate more interest."

"I think that's fine, Miss Olsen. Alfred, you can stop looking so happy. By moving on, I didn't mean to Heaven. I mean I want Miss Olsen to show me one of those new condos by the river. The ones that have the cute doorman and an elevator. Make sure it's a big one."

Elevator or doorman, I wonder?

"I would be happy to see what's available in those buildings." I chortled inwardly. Those condos were listed in the three-fifty to four-hundred-thousand-dollar range.

"Mother, I think that's an excellent idea. Miss Olsen, you may offer any potential customer a five-thousand-dollar allowance for whatever it is they think is necessary."

"That better speed things up, Olsen. Come on, Alfred, stop ogling her and let's get going. I don't want to be late for my doctor's appointment. They're slow enough as it is."

"Thank you, Mrs. Fitch and Mr. Fitch. We will see what happens. The next showing should be in just a few minutes. I'll tell the agent and his clients about the allowance. Shall I just go out the front when we're done?"

"Yes, just turn the lock on the inside and when you shut the door it will lock," Mr. Fitch said as he ushered Mother and her walker out the door.

I heard them go out through the kitchen into the garage and the sound of the car faded into the distance as the garage door came down.

I left the library and went into the living room. The space was beautifully proportioned, just like the library. The view out the long windows was spectacular. A lush green lawn bordered by perennial beds with blooms of every color just starting to peek out. Another week and this would be a showplace. Except for the boiler, electrical system and plumbing.

The doorbell rang. It wasn't so much a doorbell as an entire chorus of Westminster chimes. I went across the living room to the foyer. I peeked out the diamond-shaped window in the heavy oak front door. It was the agent and his client. I opened the door.

"Hello. You must be John. I'm Ophelia Olsen, the listing agent. Please come in."

John stepped into the foyer followed by a short blonde woman. The woman was short, the hair was not. For a moment I wondered if we were being invaded by a country-western star. She was followed by a man wearing a very shiny sport coat. He was also wearing a shiny shirt unbuttoned halfway down his chest and a lot of gold chains. The lady (using the term loosely) was wearing leopard-print Capri pants, six-inch gold heels and a rather low-cut bright pink top made from some stretchy material that was about ready to give up and stretch no more.

"Ophelia, this is Mr. Spadafora and his secretary, Miss Goldfritz."

"How do you do Mr. Spadafora, Miss Goldfritz. Please come in. John, I will be happy to accompany you through the house if you wish, or would you rather go by yourselves?"

"Thank you, Ophelia, but I think we'll take a look through and if we have any questions we'll ask you when we're finished." John said.

"That's fine. I will be down here in the living room if you need me." I smiled at the group. They set off through the living room to the kitchen.

So Miss Goldfritz was Mr. Spadafora's secretary? Then I am very probably Eleanor Roosevelt.

I walked back into the living room. I wonder if I dared sit on the couch while I'm waiting. I wouldn't want Mother Fitch to come home and find me slacking off on her furniture. I decided to chance it. I perched in a decorous fashion on the edge while John and the clients were walking through listening to him exclaim about the quality of construction and the woodwork, blah, blah, blah.

"Dy'a know how long that wall is? I wonder if my pink mohair couch will fit there? What do you think, Ralphie?" Miss Goldfritz trilled.

Ralphie, or Mr. Spadafora as we knew him, looked a trifle uncomfortable. Apparently a lot of office work was done in Mr. Spadafora's home. I wonder if Miss Goldfritz used the couch when she took dictation.

"We'll measure it, Miss Goldfritz. I happen to have my tape with me," I volunteered, getting kind of a charge out of Mr. Spadafora's cover being blown.

We measured the wall. "How long is your pink mohair couch?" I asked.

"It's a large one. It's almost eight feet long. Do you think there's room?"

"It looks like it will just fit between these windows. There is about one hundred inches from the outside of the window casing to the next window casing."

She looked disappointed. "Oh, is that enough?"

I smiled as if I meant it. "If your couch is eight feet long, there will be a few inches left over."

"Oh, good. That's a relief. Let's go look at the rest of the house. I like this place, Ralphie." They all trotted off through the end of the living room to the library accompanied by the rapid clicking of the six-inch heels.

I sat back down on the couch thinking about what a hoot it would be if the Fitches arrived home right now. Fortunately I think Mr. Fitch said the doctor's appointment wasn't until one-thirty, so they shouldn't be home for a while yet.

I got up and wandered through the dining room to the kitchen. I wanted to look around a little more without the Fitches on my tail. I opened the big built-in refrigerator. It was a commercial model with a porcelain interior and several stainless steel shelves. The outside was all stainless steel. I found the manufacturer's plate near the door hinge. This particular machine was made in 1939. Just before most of the steel went to build ships and planes for World War II. This thing must be built like a tank to have lasted all these years. It probably wasn't as efficient as the new ones but it still worked great. I think it looked to be about twice as big as mine. Almost as interesting were the contents. There was probably about 50 cubic feet in there and only six containers of food. A box of soy milk, two little pork chops that were just thawing out, a plate holding a stick of butter, a loaf of bread and a half-empty can of dog food. Assuming the pork chops were for the Fitches' dinner, I wonder who was going to finish the dog food? The can looked a little old. It either belonged to Mopsy or Mother. I shut the door quickly as I heard a noise coming from the garage. The door was opening followed by the sound of a car pulling in. They're home already. I decided to get out of the kitchen. Just as I went through the mahogany swinging door into the dining room I hear the kitchen door from the garage open and Mother Fitch's voice.

"I hope those people are gone."

"I think the cars were still out front, Mother," Alfred's voice answered her.

I was looking out the dining room windows at the gardens, trying to be nonchalant, when they came through the door.

"You still here, Olsen?"

"Yes, Mrs. Fitch, the clients are still looking at the house. They've been here a while, so they should be done shortly."

"If they've been that long, they had better buy it. I'm going to go sit down." She and the walker tottered off toward the living room.

Mr. Fitch and I followed her. Mrs. Fitch sat on the couch, in her accustomed spot, while Alfred sat in a leather wing chair and I settled into a nice puffy upholstered tapestry chair.

"So, Ophelia, are you married?" Mrs. Fitch asked.

"Not anymore." I said. Maybe that was too much information. I should have just said I was single.

"Too bad you didn't get together with old Bosch, the man that bought the house down the street. He had to send for a wife."

"Mother, Miss Olsen probably isn't interested in the neighborhood gossip. We aren't sure that's the case," Alfred chimed in.

"Hogwash, Alfred. Everybody is interested in other people's dirty little secrets. Besides, you told me about the mail-order bride yourself. Do you know old Bosch, Olsen?"

"Yes, I know who he is. He owns the cleaner shop just two blocks from my office. Occasionally he stops in for a cup of coffee." I was hoping Mother Fitch would keep blabbing. Alfred was decidedly uncomfortable at his mother's revelations of what was probably a semi-confidential locker room conversation at the golf course.

I may think better of this, but here goes. "He is getting a mail-order bride?"

"That's what he told Alfred. She's supposed to have been here by now. I don't think she's going to show up. He went and spent all kinds of money on that big house. The old fool."

"Mother, I'm sure things will work out for him. There's just been a little delay."

"Well, I think buying women from foreign countries is illegal anyway. I'll bet it is, isn't it, Olsen?"

"I really don't know anything about the laws on buying women, but I'm sure he checked into it."

"He's still an old fool. There's plenty of women right around here." With that she slammed the wizened little mouth shut and nodded off.

After a few minutes of silence from Alfred and I and some gentle snoring and an occasional sputter from Mrs. Fitch, we heard John and his clients coming down the stairs.

Miss Goldfritz, the secretary, was chattering every step of the way, with an occasional grunt from Mr. Spadafora. Their agent periodically tried to get a word in, most unsuccessfully.

The gradually increasing volume woke Mrs. Fitch from her nap. Just then the three of them came through the archway from the foyer. Mrs. Fitch's dried-apple face opened up wide at the sight of Miss Goldfritz.

"Ophelia, I think we are through now," John said to me. Turning to his clients he said, "Do either of you have any questions?"

Unfortunately, Miss Goldfritz did. "Oh, these must be the owners. How do you do? I'm Sally Goldfritz, Mr. Spadafora's secretary. This is Mr. Spadafora," she said, grabbing Ralphie's shirtsleeve. "I was just wondering if Mr. Spadafora bought the house, if you would sell that bedroom set up there in the big bedroom. I mean the one in the really big bedroom, you know, with the pink flowers on the wall?"

Alfred spoke before his mother could form any sentences from her rapidly twitching mouth. "It is possible we may want to sell some of the furniture. If you should be interested, please make a list of what you might want."

Just at that point the twitching slowed enough for Mrs. Fitch to start verbalizing her thoughts.

"Over my dead ..."

I jumped right in. "What Mrs. Fitch means is that when she's gone, she won't need any of the furniture anyway." I looked at Mother Fitch and smiled, hoping she would get the message. More sputtering noises were coming from the hole under her nose and I was afraid a word would pop out, but as I continued to smile at her, the frequency and volume started to drop.

"John, thank you for showing the house. Call me if you have any questions. Here, take one of my cards. You can call me at the office, or at home, anytime."

Sally had to get one last shot. "I just love this house. And she's so cute." That last bit was accompanied by a flashing pink fingernail about two inches long directed at Mrs. Fitch, whose eyes flew wide open and the mouth started sputtering again.

I hustled them to the front door. "Thanks again, John. I also wanted to mention to you that the sellers are going to include a five-thousand-dollar allowance for replacing the boiler or electrical work or whatever might be appropriate." I turned to the lovely couple. "It was very nice to meet you, Mr. Spadafora. Miss Goldfritz." I opened the door and they exited. I breathed a sigh of relief. Now to make my own graceful exit. I walked back into the living room.

"Secretary? He expects us to believe that?" Mrs. Fitch had finally gotten the words out. I started to laugh. Mrs. Fitch swiveled her head to look at me. I couldn't stop laughing. Unexpectedly, she broke out into a hysterical cackle that bounced off the walls and rang through the big room. Alfred's look of surprise morphed into a big smile and laughing sounds. I think Alfred needed to practice laughing. The three of us sat there and laughed out loud for several minutes. I had to wipe the tears from my cheeks. Mother Fitch had little rivers of tears running through the wrinkles in her face in gravity-defying directions.

I went over to the couch and took Mrs. Fitch's hand. "Thank you, Mrs. Fitch. I have to get back to the office. I'll call you if these people decide to do anything." I started to walk toward the door.

"Hey, Olsen."

I turned and looked back.

"I haven't had a good laugh in quite a while. Come back and we'll do it again."

I waved and went out the door.

It was after 3:30 and I decided to go straight home. I had time to use my new vacuum cleaner bags and cook some dinner before meeting Broni tonight.

13 CHAPTER THIRTEEN

Vacuuming is a good thing to do if you want time to think about things. It is not a good thing if you want to keep your mind busy so as not to have time to think about things. I spent over an hour chasing down furballs and dust bunnies and other flotsam and jetsam all over the downstairs. Since running a vacuum cleaner is not exactly rocket science, I had all that time to think about tonight.

All I know about stakeouts is what I have read in novels. I have a feeling that the people who write those novels probably have never been on a stakeout either. I do remember that Emma Peel and John Steed had champagne and probably toast points with caviar on their stakeouts. If you have toast points you probably don't call it a stakeout either. It might be an automotive soiree with vigilance.

If the truth were known, I think I am just getting scared. I don't like the idea of purposely placing my body anywhere near a person who would have no qualms about harming it. It seems to me to be an unnecessary activity. Maybe I should have just told Broni that I would not go. Maybe she would have backed down and called it off, but I don't think so. If I remember correctly, that is why I am going, because I was afraid she would go alone.

With the vacuum cleaner safely stowed away in the closet

until the next time I have an attack of cleanliness, I went into the kitchen. George and Ira were pacing the floor, wondering when I would realize it was after five o'clock. I opened a can of liver and bacon, which is one of Ira's personal favorites, and dumped it in their bowls. I fixed myself a salad and went back into the living room to watch the news. That was a mistake. Being a suburb of Buffalo, we hear a lot about their crime, which seems to be a lot more violent than ours. Tonight there were about three murders, a carjacking and an armed robbery. All things that could happen to people sitting in a car in close proximity to evildoers. I turned the news off and leaned back in the chair and shut my eyes. I need to focus and concentrate on deep breathing and clearing my mind. I took three deep breaths and decided this was for the birds.

I still had about forty-five minutes left before I had to meet Broni. I checked the batteries in the digital camera, plugged my cell phone in to charge and found my big round spotlight that plugs into the 12-volt outlet in the car. I took it out to the car and plugged it in. I packed a bag with two water bottles and a jar of peanuts. What happens after I drink the two water bottles? It's not likely that the bad guys are going to let me use the bathroom. I guess I'll cross that bridge when I come to it. I ran upstairs and changed into jeans and a sweatshirt and sneakers. I may as well look athletic.

It was time to leave. The sun was dropping down behind the skyline, which consisted of houses and trees. I figured if it was down behind the houses, it wouldn't be long before it actually fell behind the edge of the earth. I know the earth doesn't really have an edge, but since it looks like it from here, I find that a convenient way to explain the disappearance of the sun. It fits better with the idea that if the earth is a cube, now the sun is shining on the next side of the box.

I turned on my outside lights and opened the garage door.

Locking the house behind me, I went out to the garage and checked to make sure the camera, flashlight and food bag were all in the back seat. On the drive to Broni's house, I felt a frisson of excitement, much like Emma Peel must have when she is anticipating a grand adventure. My frisson quickly dissipated when I remembered that Emma also had firearms, pointy-toed boots and quite a lot of skill in the martial arts department. I had two water bottles and round-toed sneakers. Broni had her outside lights on when I pulled up in the driveway. I sat there for a minute to see if she would come out. The back door opened and out she came. Dressed all in black, with what looked to be large army boots on her feet, carrying a cloth satchel with a baguette sticking out, she looked the very epitome of what the well-dressed stakeout chick is wearing this season.

She opened the back door and deposited her bag on the seat, then got in the passenger side. She didn't speak until the door was shut and she had her seat belt on. That took a moment because of the voluminous layers of clothing. I was still staring at her when she turned her head. "Good evening, Oph. If you are you ready, let us go."

"I think so. There's just one minor point I need to know. Where are we going?"

Broni broke out in a big grin. She was really enjoying this.

"Oh, that's right. I think we should start by parking near Aunt Laima's house. That's where Mikelis was last seen."

"So what does this guy look like?"

"Oh, you will recognize him. He looks like George Clooney, but younger and only has one hand."

"No problem, a young George Clooney I can recognize, but we probably can't see his hand from here anyway. Maybe he has a prosthetic hand by now. One other thing, what if he should walk by the car? How do we explain us sitting here in the evening watching him? Have we thought of this?"

"We will be parked down the street from Laima's house. She is not home. She works at night, so she cannot see us. If anyone should come down the sidewalk by the car we will pretend we are reading a map."

"And what if he decides to help two lost females reading a map by knocking on the window and offering us directions?"

"Oph, you are worrying too much. If he is involved in criminal activities, he will not stop to help us. He will be in a hurry to get to his next crime. Now please start driving."

"Ok, which direction?"

"Turn left at the corner right here and go until you get to Ottawa Street. Then we will go right about half a block. Laima's house is at the end of the first block of Ottawa."

I backed out of Broni's driveway and followed her instructions. We pulled up to the curb about halfway down Laima's block. The street was narrow and lined with what looked like two-family houses. The front lawns were shallow, which made the street seem even narrower. The houses were tall and narrow. Probably most of them had an apartment downstairs and one up. I stopped the car.

"What now? Do you notice how narrow the street is? If anyone walked past us they could see our faces."

"Relax, Oph. The people in this neighborhood mind their own business. It's too dangerous to be looking at other people. You might see something you shouldn't."

"Yeah, like us sitting in a car."

"It's dark now. There won't be that many people out anyway."

I slunk down in my seat. The fact that stakeouts are boring became immediately evident. We sat there silently for about ten minutes. Not a soul stirred within sight. I was wondering if I dared drink my water. I was most certainly not going to ask anyone here to use their ladies' room.

All of a sudden, Broni reached around into the back seat and whipped a road map out of her bag. She made a great show of opening it and thrusting part of it under my nose. The edge caught my lip and my head jerked back into the head rest.

"What are you ..."

"Ssh," Broni hissed at me, followed loudly by, "which road do you think we should take to get to Batavia?"

"I don't give a damn which road you ..." I looked over at the passenger's side window just then and saw a young, rather good-looking man on the sidewalk. He was glancing in our direction. Fortunately the road map pretty well obscured our faces. He was walking rather hurriedly. As he passed with his arms swinging, I could see the too-bright pink of a prosthetic hand. He was dressed in a suit and tie. Hardly the outfit for the casual criminal.

He was past the car in a matter of seconds. I whispered to Broni. "Was that him?"

She shook her head up and down and whispered back. "Yes, I am sure it was. Did you see the plastic hand?"

"Yes. I did. Where is he going now?"

I pushed the map down a little to see in the rear-view mirror. It was dark now, but I could just see him as he reached the next street light.

"He's still walking. How do we find out where he's going?" I asked Broni.

"We will turn around in that driveway up ahead and then follow him." She beamed.

"Broni, this is for real, let me remind you. He may be armed and desperate. Do you propose that we just trail along behind him in the car and hope he doesn't notice?"

"No, just turn around and proceed up to the next corner slowly. Maybe he will go somewhere by then. If he doesn't, then we go around the block. It will work. Hurry."

I moved the car forward and pulled into the next driveway. I backed out, facing the other direction and we moved slowly up the street. Broni kept her eye on Mikelis. He was halfway down the next block when we reached the corner.

"What now, Sherlock?"

"Keep going. We are far enough behind that he isn't paying any attention to us."

I kept on going, looking around for another side street or some means of escape if he should spot us. I didn't see any.

"Look," Broni exclaimed, swinging her arms around.

Mikelis had turned into a doorway. I sped up a little. When we reached the spot where he disappeared we saw a little neighborhood bar.

I stopped the car about two houses down from the bar. "Now what?" I hissed.

"I don't know," Broni hissed back.

"What do you mean you don't know? Didn't your plan cover this contingency?"

"Let me think for a minute. That place belongs to Laima's brother-in-law. It is a neighborhood tavern. Mostly the foundry workers go there. I think he and his wife live upstairs."

"Ok, so Mikelis could have been going to the bar or he could have gone upstairs to the apartment? Perhaps we could just disguise ourselves as foundry workers and wander in. We could perch on bar stools and order beer in Livonian."

Broni looked at me with a combination of pity and forbearance. "Have you gone plumb loco?" Back to the Western patois.

"No, not plumb, a little slanted perhaps. Never mind. I guess we have come to a dead end. My point is, there's no way we can find out what's going on in there."

"Maybe we could find out a little bit. We could visit Laima and ask about her family." Broni looked very pleased with herself.

"Oh, that will be subtle. I don't even know this woman and I'm asking her about her family?"

"No, you won't be. We will just happen to be in the neighborhood and stop to see her. I will ask about the relatives."

"You said she works nights, so we can't do it now anyway. Besides, I think we are getting in just a little over our heads. Detective Crowley said to quietly ask around, not stake out bars."

"Don't worry, Oph. Oh, look here he comes."

I swung my head around in a non-professional manner and looked back at the bar. Mikelis had walked out the front door and turned down the sidewalk in the direction he came from.

"Oh, Oph, turn around and follow him."

"Wait a minute, here. Isn't he going to get just a little suspicious of this car showing up every place he does? And isn't he going to get my license number and track me down and torture me?"

She looked defeated.

I went forward about another three houses before turning into a driveway and backing out again, heading in the same direction as our prey. I stepped on the gas and then stopped at the first corner's stop sign. There was nothing coming in the other directions, so I stepped on the gas again and went down the street, passing Mikelis.

"What are you doing? Have you lost your senses?" Broni whispered, quite loudly.

"No, but if I keep driving behind him slowly, he is going to catch on pretty soon that we're following him. And don't forget, he looked right at the car when he walked past us the first time."

She didn't look convinced. We continued down the street and turned right at the next corner. I pulled over to the curb so that my car was hidden by one in back of it. When Mikelis passed by the corner, he wouldn't be able to see us.

"Now look in the mirrors to see when he passes the corner," I told her.

We both watched out our respective side-view mirrors, when much to our simultaneous horror, Mikelis turned at the corner and came down the sidewalk toward the car.

"Get out the map again, quick!" I said. Broni started thrashing around on the floor. Her boots were so big, they pretty much obscured anything that may have been down there. She lurched forward and grabbed the corner of the map. Unfortunately, one of the boots was firmly ensconced upon another corner. She yanked upward and the map came up with a big boot-shaped hole in it. She put it up over her face and I tried to hide behind the edge. We watched through the hole as Mikelis walked past the car. He glanced over for a second, looked back at the sidewalk, then swung his head back in our direction. We both held our breath and dared not peek through the hole. Finally the sound of his hard-soled shoes hitting the concrete picked up speed again and we were able to resume breathing. I peeked around the edge of the map and saw him walking down the street, already about four houses away.

"Broni, is it alright with you if my heart starts up again? That was a little close. He has to be wondering just how stupid we are to have only gotten two blocks after looking at a map."

I looked over at her. She was peeking over the top of the map watching the suspect disappear around the next corner.

She turned her head. For the first time I think I saw a little glimmer of fright.

"Are you beginning to understand how dangerous this could be? We don't know what he is involved in. I am not really Emma Peel. I just pretend to be in my less lucid moments. Let's go home now."

"No, Oph. We cannot. We have to follow him. We know he

came from a house near Laima's. He went into the bar. Now he is going somewhere else. They all have to be connected somehow. Drive the car."

"Drive the car where? Don't you think the next time he sees us, he might start to pound on the window and ask what we think we are doing? What do you want to tell him? That we were going to the town that got ripped out of the map and we just have to go two blocks at a time?"

"No, no, he will not see us. Let's just go to the end of the block to see where he is going."

Much against my better judgment, I pulled out of the parking space and proceeded to the end of the block. I stopped just short of the corner.

"Move up, Oph, move! I can't see around the corner."

I snuck forward a little so she could see around the corner.

"Look, Oph. There he goes. He just got on that bus! Follow it!"

Sure enough. We saw Mikelis stepping up into the Ottawa street bus, and the bus pulling away.

"Where does that bus go?" I asked, hoping she would know.

"I think it goes down Ottawa, then over Klamath to Main. I don't know where it goes after that."

"Ok, we have a few minutes before he is probably going to get off. I have an idea!" I looked at Broni cheerfully. "Let's go to your house and get your car. He's seen this one two or three times tonight. If we are sitting at the bus stop when he gets off, I cannot imagine what uncivilized thoughts may go traipsing through his head."

As I was talking, I was following the bus, but turned off about two blocks from Broni's house.

"See, we are almost there and we can get your car and beat the bus over to Main and Klamath to see if he gets off."

She opened her mouth a couple of times to protest, but my uninterruptible monologue and the fact that I was now pulling into her driveway rendered any objection moot.

"Ok, I have my keys in my purse. Pull up on the side of my car so we can get out."

She jumped out of the car and opened the door to the Megaton Monster. I pulled my car up beside hers, shut it off and got out. She had the Monster revved up and ready to go, so I jumped in the passenger's side. We tore out of her little driveway as though we knew where we were going and what we were doing. It only took about four minutes to cut across Klamath toward Main. As she turned onto Klamath, we saw the bus three vehicles ahead of us. As it pulled up to the bus stop on Main, we watched carefully as two people got off, then a third. It was Mikelis. Broni pulled over to the curb. We were far enough back and in a different vehicle, so I wasn't worried about him recognizing us.

"What is he doing? He's just standing there," I mused out loud.

"I don't know. Maybe he is waiting for someone to pick him up."

We had our answer shortly. Within about two minutes, another bus came along. The Main Street bus.

"So where does the Main bus go?" I asked.

Broni looked at me like I was from Mars.

"Oph, did you not ever take a bus?"

"Well, maybe once, a long time ago."

"The Main Street bus goes toward Colcott Avenue, then east toward the University."

"What would a potential evildoer be doing going in that direction? Follow that bus!"

Broni pulled out of the parking spot and followed my orders. The ones that were issued in a fit of temporary insanity. We followed that bus up Main Street. Broni was right; it turned onto Colcott and came to a bus stop. The doors opened and

Mikelis got off. In the meantime Broni had swerved to the right, coming to rest against the curb when she saw the bus stop.

"Now I know what these grab bars above the windows are for," I gasped as I righted myself.

Broni looked over. "I thought those were to hang clothes on."

"Keep an eye on the suspect, please," I said.

"He is standing on the curb, waiting for something. I don't think any other buses come this way."

"There he goes. He's crossing the street. We'll just have to stay here until he gets farther away."

Broni protested. "What if he gets out of eyesight?"

"If he starts to look real tiny like he's very far away, then we can move. Ok?"

She shook her head up and down in reluctant agreement.

Mikelis walked down Colcott until he came to the corner of Southampton Court, where he took a left and disappeared from sight.

"Now can we go, Miss Emma Peel?" Broni said with a perceptible air of frustration.

"It's Mrs. Peel to you and yes, we can go," I said in my best semi-Peel accent.

The Brobdingnagian Behemoth crept out of the parking space, having had to wait for a passing car.

"Hurry up, you American tourist," Broni hissed as the offending auto crawled by us. It too turned onto Southampton Court. I recognized the driver. It was Alfred Fitch. Mother was in the car and they were toodling along about 15 miles per hour.

"Broni, that was no tourist. It was Mr. Fitch of my Southampton Court listing. He just likes to drive at a leisurely pace."

"That is not necessary when I am hot on the trail of a perp."

"A perp? Is that anything like a twerp?"

At that she gave me a disgusted look and continued growling

at the Fitch car. I looked down the street and spotted Mikelis walking along rapidly as though he knew where he was going.

"Relax, Broni. There's our prey, up ahead about five houses. What could he be doing in this neighborhood? I got the idea his usual haunts were on the other side of town. This may explain why he is dressed nicely."

The Fitch car turned into their driveway and proceeded slowly up the long driveway. I was shocked to see the big old garage door slowly ascend as they approached it. I didn't suspect Mother Fitch would want to get into anything as high-tech as a garage door opener.

In the meantime, we continued down the street, Broni keeping her big reindeer eye on the suspect. I don't think Emma Peel would have said "perp," so I shan't either.

One of my big concerns was that even though we were in a different car, wouldn't Mikelis have to be a real dim bulb to not notice two cars following him slowly in one night? We were creeping along almost as slowly as Alfred Fitch had. We both yelled at once.

"There he goes into a driveway!" yelled Broni.

"That's Mr. Bosch's house!" yelled me.

We pulled over to the right, up against the curb, but with a softer landing this time.

"What business does Mikelis have with Mr. Bosch?" I asked, not quite believing it.

"Mr. Bosch seems like such a nice man. Why is he consorting with criminal types?" Broni said sadly.

We both sat silently for a few minutes. Probably because neither one of us knew what to do next.

"We certainly can't go pounding on the door and asking what's going on." I looked over at Broni. She had a peculiar look on her face. "No, we can't and that's final."

"No, Oph. We don't go to the door. We could just walk

around the outside and perhaps linger at a window."

"Are you out of your mind? We could get arrested or beaten up or something. The neighbors would call the police in a minute if they saw us."

"Oph, look at Mr. Bosch's side yard. It is covered with trees. The trees go all the way back to Colcott Avenue. All we have to do is park the car around the corner and walk through the trees and we will be back here! It is simple."

"No, you are simple and so am I if I agree to this."

As she was speaking, she was driving down Southampton and following the bend around that brought us back to Colcott. She turned right and pulled up to the curb.

"Broni, this is insane. If anyone sees us, it will be the end of my career and possibly my ability to walk and talk at the same time."

There was no stopping her. She didn't even answer me. She got out of the truck and as nonchalantly as possible when you're a six-foot-two female, sauntered onto the sidewalk and looked around. She gestured impatiently at me to hurry. I said a very quick prayer and got out and joined her.

"Now be very quiet," she warned me.

"Don't worry. I'm not carrying on any conversations with anybody."

She shushed me again with a finger to her lips.

We went off the sidewalk across the grass and back through the trees. I was wondering who owned this land. I didn't think Mr. Bosch's lot would come back this far. It looked like maybe a common area or a piece left over that was too small to build on. We only had to walk about 75 feet before we came to the edge of the thick trees. Beyond lay Mr. Bosch's lawn. There were a few trees on it, but nowhere as thick as what we had just come through. If anyone looked out the window, they could see us.

I poked Broni. "Now what?"

She turned around and bent down to whisper. "We go to some windows to listen. Now be quiet."

We snuck across the lawn approaching the side of the house. Most of these houses have their living rooms toward the front, opposite the front entry door. I tugged on Broni's sleeve and pointed at the window I thought had the greatest likelihood of being a living room. We stole up to the window and paused. I whispered, "Nothing."

We went to the next window, about twenty feet further. As we approached, there were the sounds of two voices. One was recognizable as Mr. Bosch. The other was very heavily accented and came from a younger man. The voices were getting louder. Mr. Bosch was doing most of the yelling. The other voice got deeper and louder. It was very hard to distinguish what they were saying other than the words, "no more" from Mr. Bosch, then "get out." The yelling continued, but sounded farther away. We stood very quietly, not moving a muscle. I crept a little closer to the window and tried to stretch myself up over the sill to see inside. I saw a large room with Mr. Bosch and Mikelis yelling at each other. The yelling sounded farther away because Mr. Bosch was persuading Mikelis toward the front door by waving a golf club at him. He took a couple of swings, but the younger man was too fast for him and took off toward the door.

We heard the door slam and decided at this point we had better run. We turned toward the woods and the thought of Mikelis being outside the house spurred us on to greater speed. More speed than caution, unfortunately, as Broni slammed into a young maple that had a great capacity for flexibility. If it hadn't bent at a right angle, it would have broken. She unwrapped her arms and legs from the trunk and took off again. I was, by this time, about halfway through the woods, but stopped and turned around to see if Broni was alright. She had started running again by then, but I also saw what appeared to be the figure of Mikelis running down Southampton. Fortunately the street was far enough away that he paid no attention to the ruckus going on at the edge of the wooded area. We kept on going until we reached the safety of the Bronimobile.

We were both out of breath. "Unlock the doors, hurry."

"I am trying. The keys are under two layers of pants. Here they are."

She unlocked the doors and we flew up into the seats, slammed the doors and locked them just in time to look up and see a man running around the other corner of Southampton and Colcott.

"Broni, there he goes. What do we do now? Do we call the police?"

"Why would we call the police? Mr. Bosch was the one swinging the club. Let's just see where he goes." She started the engine and we crept forward. Mikelis stayed on the same side of Colcott.

"Broni, stay back. He isn't going anywhere. Do you suppose he's waiting for the bus again?"

She pulled over to the curb, just a short distance from where we were before. Just then, a bus came down Colcott from the east. It stopped at the next corner and Mikelis got on.

"How did he know when the next bus was coming?" I asked in all sincerity.

Broni gave me look of pity. "Oph, I think it was an accident that he got here at the right time. It didn't look like his departure was timed."

"Oh, right. I guess we assume he is going back to the house he first came out of. At least we don't have to follow him anymore."

Broni got that strange look in her eye again.

"No. We are not going to follow him anymore. We are done.

That's it. The only thing I will be a part of is driving past Mr. Bosch's house to see if we can tell if he's alright. Go down to the corner and turn right. That's an order." I didn't really know if telling Broni something was an order was going to work, but it did. We went to the stop sign at the corner and she started to turn right.

We rounded the corner where Southampton curves and continued to Mr. Bosch's house. As we passed, we saw Mr. Bosch standing in the driveway talking to someone. "I wonder if a neighbor showed up after hearing the noise?" I asked Broni. She grunted.

Broni continued driving and came around the second curve that brought us back onto Colcott. She turned right toward Main Street. I hoped we were going back to her house.

"Are we done yet?" I asked hopefully. I put my head back on the seat and closed my eyes. This detective stuff is tiring and I should have worn more layers of clothing. A girl could get chilled running around in the woods after dark.

"Yes. We will go back to my house and you can get your car. Then you can go home and get your beauty sleep. That's what you call it, right?" She laughed.

"Yes, that's what I call it and I'll thank you not to laugh. One of these days it will work."

After a few minutes we were back at Broni's house. I stumbled out of the seat and dug my car keys out of my purse.

"Thanks for the adventure. I am going home."

"We have much pondering to do, Oph. Go get your beauty sleep and I'll see you in the morning."

14 CHAPTER FOURTEEN

The morning dawned. That's about the best thing I could say for it. My poor old body was stiff and sore from the night before and my bed was so cozy with the blankets and the comforter and two cats on top lined up alongside my left leg. Needless to say, I had to drag myself forcibly out of bed and run to the bathroom. I wouldn't have done this until later, but I was supposed to be at the office at nine o'clock to answer the phones. The running is not so much for the physical fitness aspect as it is to prevent myself from freezing to death on the way. Big old houses tend to have cold spots in them. Actually "spots" isn't quite accurate. It's more like entire rooms. I try to pay as little of my money to the gas company as is humanly possible. In the spring, it is very tricky because the nights are still cold and the days are warmer. Getting the temperature adjusted to not provide much heat in the daytime and keep it above freezing at night takes some doing.

I managed to bathe and dress without icicles forming on any part of my body and make my way to the kitchen. George and Ira thundered down the stairs ahead of me so as to be able to sit on the kitchen floor and howl as if they had never eaten while I filled their bowls. I microwaved some old coffee, took my pills and used the lukewarm sludge to wash down a handful of bran flakes.

"See you later," I yelled to the cats and ran for the door, grabbing my briefcase and purse along the way. On the way out to the garage I started to think about how I really don't bear any resemblance to Emma Peel. I mean, think about it. I can't get out of bed in the morning, I stumble around, I fly out the door at the last minute and punch the garage door opener while meandering down the sidewalk to the garage.

In severe contrast, Emma probably emerges from her bed perfectly made up, wearing a very glamorous nightgown that most likely resembles her daytime outfit, waltzes into her bath chamber, sinking into a tub full of lightly scented bubbles, emerges like "The Birth of Venus" and slips effortlessly into the black Spandex suit and pointy-toed boots. After that, the butler serves a light breakfast and Emma's camouflaged garage door rises as she slips into the baby-blue Lotus Elan for another day of crime fighting. I don't need to elaborate on the differences.

I backed my non-conspicuous auto out of the uncamouflaged garage and motored to the office. I presume Emma Peel would "motor" as opposed to "drive."

The first thing I noticed was the strange car in the parking lot. It was kind of early for customers to be wandering in. The only other car in the parking lot was Broni's. Maybe it was somebody dropping off contracts or other papers. I pushed the front door open and went in to the lobby. I turned right to go into my office and set my things down and went back out and down the hall to Broni's office. As I approached the door I realized who the plain gray car in the parking lot belonged to. I should have remembered it from the last visit.

"Good morning, Detective Crowley. Nice to see you again. Oh, please don't get up." Hubert Crowley was sitting in a chair in front of Broni's desk and had no intention of getting up. I walked around to the other side of the chair so I was facing him. He didn't look happy. Neither did Broni.

"Good morning, Ms. Olsen. I was just asking Ms. Z if she

had had any success with her inquiries. She told me about your little adventure last evening."

Ok. Do I pretend I have a sudden case of amnesia or do I go along with this? Seeing as how Broni has already spilled the beans, I have no choice but to cheerfully respond.

"Oh, she did?" I said in one of my most charming tones of voice. The assumption being that I have more than one tone of voice, and that at least one of them is charming. Presuming this is all true, Crowley should have responded in a more civil manner.

"Yes, she did. Ms. Olsen, did it occur to you at any point last night that you could be putting yourselves or other people in danger?"

Broni hung her head like a chastened child while I thought of several different approaches to this. My first thought was one of unfairness. He has been sitting here talking to Broni and did he yell at her like this? No, he waited for me. I thought I had best respond with something intelligent, and, I might add, I shall not be wasting my charming tone of voice on him. I shall use one of the lesser tones. Maybe he was just waiting for both of us to be together so he wouldn't have to yell twice. Since the adventure was Broni's idea, why was I worried about making excuses? I was just along for the ride. I looked at Broni. She still had her head down. I think somewhere in that large skull, she had assumed the police would be grateful for her expert help. It now appeared the opposite was true. I guess I'd better try to defend her.

"Detective Crowley, we were merely observing a gentleman whose name was brought up during a conversation with one of Broni's friends. We had asked about unusual happenings and strange people coming into town just as you had asked us to. This gentleman is known to the person with whom we were having the conversation. Her observation was that the gentleman was up to no good. We just assumed that having us stealthily keep an eye on his movements could possible be helpful to your investigation."

As I talked, Crowley's brows gradually furrowed closer and closer until they were one. Now I know why his name is Bert. I wondered where Ernie was.

"Miss Olsen, the police department is extremely grateful for your assistance." At this Broni perked up, but not for long. Actually I detected just a hint of sarcasm in his statement. "However, we are charged with the duty of protecting the citizens. This becomes difficult when the citizens insist on prancing around following persons who could possibly be engaged in criminal activities. It is also possible that you could have jeopardized the official investigations that are being conducted even as we speak. Not just ours, but the Latvian Embassy inquiry into the possible murder of one of their people. The gentleman in question could have been alerted to the fact that certain people and agencies are interested in his presence here. Do you see what I mean?"

"Yes, of course we do. But I would like to assure you that we used every precaution to make sure the suspect did not know we were watching him. We even went so far as to change vehicles during the evening."

I could swear that his eyes actually rolled back a little. "Ms. Olsen, using tactics learned from watching TV cops will not get you far. Our people have training in the methods of observation. I can only assume that this was your first foray into the world of surveillance?"

I looked at Broni to see if she was going to respond. She seemed not to be able to say anything, so once again I ventured forth.

"Yes, it was the first time I have been involved in this sort of thing. I have to admit we are not as well-trained as your people."

Detective Crowley took a deep breath. "Please consider yourselves duly warned. I do not want you doing any more of this in the future. If necessary, I will take steps to see that you do not. Including putting you in protective custody in our Village facility."

Broni's eyes got very large. So did mine. I think we had just been threatened with incarceration in the local hoosegow.

Detective Crowley continued, "Now, while I do not want to encourage you two, I would like to know what you saw last night."

Broni sat up straight and lost her hangdog look. She was being asked to brief a detective. The stuff of her dreams. Broni proceeded to tell him everything, even the fact that she had purposely concealed the information we got from Aija. "Is Mr. Bosch going to be in trouble?" I asked.

Crowley looked at me, "There hasn't been any report of a beating by a three wood. There isn't too much I can do at the moment and I don't want to tip off anyone just yet."

"Mikelis didn't look like he was hurt. He was running and stood at the bus stop pretty normally. He straightened up his suit coat and tie," I added.

"Suit coat?" Crowley was interested. "He was dressed up? That's interesting. However, ladies, please listen to what I said. I do not want you anywhere near these people. You could get hurt, get someone else hurt or jeopardize the investigation. Stick to real estate. Good afternoon."

With that, he left.

"Well, I guess that's the end of that, isn't it?" I said to Broni.

She sat there staring straight ahead. I think it was difficult for her to adjust to the fact that the police department did not seem to want her help. All those hours in front of the TV wasted.

"I wonder if we got Mr. Bosch into trouble?" she said after a moment.

"Crowley didn't say so. Is it a crime to swing a golf club at somebody? I don't think he hit him."

"We had to tell him everything. It might help them catch Mikelis or at least find out what he is doing."

I walked around to the front of the desk. "Now, Broni. This has to be the end of our involvement in this stuff. You heard Crowley. He says we could get hurt or cause someone else to get hurt. What if Mikelis recognized you last night. He might go to Aija and try to get information out of her about why you were following him or what you know about him. He could hurt her or the kids. I think it is time we just left all this to the police. I am not cut out for this, my Emma Peel fantasies notwithstanding."

Broni looked up at me. "What was Mikelis doing at Mr. Bosch's house?"

I rolled my eyes. "Broni, it is none of our business. We told the detective about Mikelis. That is all we were asked to do."

"Oph, aren't you wondering what the connection is?"

"No. I shall assume Mikelis' vacuum cleaner was acting up and he was consulting with Mr. Bosch about possible repairs. Obviously the conversation became heated and Mr. Bosch decided to put the vacuum cleaner out of its misery with a hit to the bag area."

Now it was Broni who rolled her eyes. "Mikelis was not carrying a vacuum cleaner on the bus. You are being insane. We found out more in one night than the police have in a week."

"Broni, I have to admit, I am a little curious about the connections between the various people in this mystery but I also have a very high regard for my own skin. I would not like to see it endangered in any way. Let's just stick to the job we were assigned. Talk to Laima if you must. See if she knows anything about the nefarious doings of her ex-nephew-in-law or whatever he is."

"Ok. Will you go with me?"

"When do you want to go?" I heard myself say this, against my better judgment. Presuming I had judgment of any kind left at this point.

"I will call Laima and see if she is working this evening. If she is off, can you go tonight?"

"Ok, see if she is going to be home. I have one appointment late this afternoon, then I'll be going home. Don't you need some excuse to visit and explain why you are dragging along a stranger? Now, I have to get back to the front desk and answer the phone."

Broni looked very pleased with herself. Why am I going with her to talk to Laima? I guess it couldn't hurt. Actually we were only doing what Detective Crowley asked us to. As long as we didn't get involved in following anybody, we would be within the letter of his request and presumably not endanger ourselves or anyone else.

I got up to the front of the office in time to see Mr. Bosch going past the front windows. I shot through the front door and practically knocked him down. I screeched to a halt right in front of him, scaring him only slightly and chirped, "Good morning, Mr. Bosch. How are you?"

He was able to speak after he regained his composure. "Fine, Oph, and how are you?"

His tone of voice was rather flat and he was not smiling. Of course, being nearly knocked down could have caused this.

"Well, I'm just fine. Why don't you come in and have a cup of coffee? Your store doesn't open for another twenty minutes."

He sidestepped and tried to get around me. That is not easy. He didn't sidestep wide enough to escape. I took his arm. "Come on, the coffee isn't that bad and we've missed you." I managed to get the door open and practically manhandle him through it.

"Oph, I really have to get to the store. I have a shipment coming in this morning and I don't want to miss it," he said as I was propelling him forward.

"Broni, look who's here. Our old friend Mr. Bosch here to have a quick cup of coffee," I yelled down the hallway.

Broni popped out of her office and said, "Hello, Mr. Bosch. Long time, no see."

"I can only stay a minute. I need to get to the store." Mr. Bosch was still protesting his kidnapping.

"Here's a nice cup of coffee, just the way you like it." Broni handed him the biggest mug we had.

He took it and sat down. I think he was beginning to get the idea that there was no use resisting.

The two of us took chairs on each side of him. He looked alarmed. I realized that we needed to cool it a little. We were acting slightly goofy.

"Ladies, I appreciate your attentiveness. What is the occasion?"

Broni looked at me and I looked down at the floor.

Finally I said, "We just haven't seen you for quite a while. How's your golf game?"

Broni rolled her eyes upward. I got the message.

"It's fine, Oph. I just haven't been able to practice as much as I'd like."

"Now, the last time I saw you, you said you were engaged. Are you ready to tell us about that?"

Mr. Bosch put down his coffee cup and said, "I really must get to the store. I can't miss the truck."

He literally ran down the hall and out the front door while Broni and I just looked at each other.

"I guess I pushed a button with that one."

"Hoo, hoo, I guess you did. He ran out of here like a skunk with his pants on fire."

I wonder what Western that was from? I think it lost a little in the translation.

"The subject of his upcoming nuptials seems to cause some level of distress. Was that it or is he just nervous and jerky because of his visitor and the ensuing altercation last night? Or is it both? Could Mikelis have a connection with the missing bride?"

Broni got up from her chair and walked around the corner and down the hallway. She walked up to the front of the office. She stopped and turned. "Maybe that is it. Maybe Mikelis does have something to do with the bride."

I leaned on the front desk with my head down in my hands. "Mrs. Fitch called Mr. Bosch a besotted old fool. She said the bride would never get here. From where? No one has said where the bride is coming from. Mr. Bosch told me that she wasn't here yet, but would be arriving in about two weeks. What if the bride is coming from Latvia? What if Mikelis is bringing her here or sending for her?"

Broni stood staring out the window and said, "But why would Mr. Bosch threaten Mikelis? He must have been extremely upset to do that. What about the bride could have made him that upset?"

"This doesn't make sense. Why would Mr. Bosch want to have a bride come from another country? Wouldn't he want someone he knew? Mrs. Fitch called her a mail-order bride. At the time I didn't take it too seriously."

I sat down at the front desk. Broni started pacing the floor in front of the window. Fortunately no one else was in the office yet.

Broni finally spoke. "Something must have gone wrong with the deal. Mikelis must be having a problem getting the bride."

I thought about this for a moment. "Maybe Mikelis told Bosch all he could get was a real ugly one?"

Broni gave me a rather disgusted look. "He certainly would

have seen a picture of her."

"Well, you would think so. I would also think that he would have corresponded with her in some way if he is going to marry her. Also, Mrs. Fitch mentioned buying the bride. I wonder if you actually have to pay for them."

"Well, of course you do. I remember back in the old country there was a girl in the village who was bought by someone in Canada and she left and no one ever saw her again," Broni enlightened me.

"Oh. I am not conversant with the protocols involved in purchasing humans. Is this not illegal? Maybe we should call Detective Crowley. Perhaps he will now recognize my brilliance for what it is. Inner beauty, as opposed to the outward kind."

Broni looked confused at my ramblings, but said, "I think we should talk to Laima before we talk to the detective. She may have some information or have heard of this kind of thing happening."

"Ok. Have you called her yet?"

As she turned to go to her office, Broni said, "I will go do it right now."

I turned my attention to the telephone. It was not ringing. Therefore I had nothing to answer. So I decided to just ponder the present situation. What did we know? Not much. We assumed some things. One being that Mikelis had some connection to Mr. Bosch's missing bride. It was beginning to look more likely. What other connection would a vacuum store owner have with a Latvian crook? We also might suppose that Mr. Bosch doesn't know that Mikelis is a crook. That would explain Mikelis being dressed up last night. The attempt to tee up Mikelis' head may have come about when Mr. Bosch found out that he was not involved with a legitimate businessman.

The morning went by with a few phone calls from window shoppers. These are people that have seen "For Sale" signs on houses but have some resistance to talking to the mortgage people to get pre-qualification letters. Usually there is a good reason. Like a bankruptcy they forgot to mention or fifteen credit cards, all maxed out. Or an enormous car payment that takes up sixty percent of their income. None of the phone calls resulted in any decent prospects. I finished up the paperwork for my listing appointment this afternoon and put it in my briefcase.

The next floor time agent came in about noon. It was the new girl, Nancy.

"Hi," she said in her terminally cheerful chirp.

"Hi, Nancy, how are you?"

"I'm fine. I'm looking forward to talking to all the nice people on the phone today. It is really fun."

"That's nice. Just make sure they have some money, a job and good credit before you waste much time on them."

"Oh, I didn't think of that."

I stopped myself from rolling my eyes again.

Walking down the hallway to Broni's office, I wondered about this whole thing. Is there any downside to talking to Laima? Are we putting ourselves in danger? My answers to myself seemed to reflect the idea that this was not as stupid as last night and couldn't be as dangerous.

"Broni, I'm leaving. Did you talk to Laima?"

"Oh, yes. She will be happy to have us come. She is off tonight and is doing some baking today. Laima is a wonderful baker. Back in Valdgale she worked in a little bakery. I don't remember much about it. I was a small child, but I remember how good the little cakes were. I haven't had any in a long time."

"Ok, what time should I come to your house?"

"Laima says to come about 6:30. Come to my house a few minutes before that."

I turned to go toward the front door. "I'll be there. See you later."

The afternoon passed uneventfully. I went on an appointment and listed a small Cape Cod in the village. The seller was a little old lady who had lived there for 50 years and still thought the gall-bladder green plastic tiles on the kitchen wall were the cat's pajamas. I just had to skirt the issue and try to introduce the concept that some people might not be entirely attuned to her decorating and that she shouldn't be shocked by that. But I did have to address the issue that these same people might not want to pay top dollar and then spend a lot of money redecorating. We kind of understood each other by the end of the meeting. As I left I wondered again why I stayed in this business.

I was driving down Main on my way home, thinking about tonight. How much could we learn from Laima? It didn't sound like she was averse to seeing us. Of course, she thought this was a purely social visit. What would happen when we started asking questions? If I remember correctly, she is Aija's aunt, not Mikelis'. I would think that would make her a little hostile toward Mikelis, after what he did to Aija.

As I passed the last big intersection before my turn to go home, I glanced out the side window. Standing on the corner was a rather familiar-looking handsome guy. I am not opposed to taking a glance at handsome guys now and again, but this was Mikelis. I looked straight ahead again and then shot another glance out the side window. He was looking right at my car. He was standing at a bus stop so he was unfortunately very close to the street. As I went across the intersection, I looked in my side mirror and saw him continue to watch me. I sped up a little and continued up the street. I turned right, then left onto my street. I was too far away for him to see where I turned, but the incident rattled me a little. Did he recognize the car from last night? And maybe he even recognized me even though I had my head down behind a map? This was not good.

I pulled up my driveway and opened the garage door. Or cave, as in Emma Peel's case. I put the car in the garage. I usually left it out if I was going out again, but I didn't want to take the chance on anyone seeing it. Perhaps this is a little paranoid, but I don't know where Mikelis was going. He was carrying a couple of bags so he could have come out of the drugstore on the corner or the grocery store next to it. He was probably just waiting for the bus to take him back to the neighborhood where he was staying, but a good detective doesn't leave the outcome to chance. I think I read that somewhere. It sounds good anyway.

I entered the kitchen to a chorus of chirps and meeoows. It wasn't anywhere near dinner time, but that didn't stop them from trying.

"Hi, guys. It's not dinnertime yet. I am going to do some work first."

I decided to finish the paperwork for the listing I had just gotten and not wait for morning. Lately, the mornings in the office were a little unpredictable. What with tripping over dead bodies and being interrogated and chastised by police detectives, our mornings were getting downright exciting.

I was sitting at the dining room table trying to concentrate on filling out the computer worksheet but the sunlight streaming in the window from the backyard was making it difficult. I decided I had to go outside.

I looked into the living room as I left the dining room going into the kitchen. George and Ira were flopped over on their backs with their paws up over their heads, lying in sun puddles on the Oriental rug. It looked like a miniature elephant graveyard.

The sky was a clear bright beautiful shade of deep blue. A few cottony clouds scattered themselves here and there. How could there be dead guys lying on the sidewalk and crooks getting shot at by little old men on such a glorious day? Of course, not all that stuff happened today, but close enough. Emma Peel never seemed to be bothered by all the crime going on around her. I think this would cause me to be upset if I had to be around murders and murderers. It isn't nearly as glamorous in person as it is in books or on TV. I wandered around the yard picking up branches and twigs that had blown off the trees over the winter. The little bundles got wrapped in twine and parked on top of the wood pile in back of the garage.

The sun started sinking behind the big pine tree at the back of the yard, which gave me a clue that it was probably after five. I piled up my last bundle and headed for the house.

The Gershwin brothers were waiting at the door. I fed them and warmed up some of my never-ending stock of chicken soup.

The kitchen clock said it was about five after six. I had better wash my face and comb my hair and start for Broni's house.

I pulled into the driveway just before 6:30. I opened the driver's door on my car just as Broni came bounding out of her house and down the steps. I stood up and yelled. "Hold it!"

She stopped in mid-stride about halfway across the lawn.

"We are not going in my car."

Her eyes got wide, "Why not? It is in the driveway in back of mine."

"Two reasons. Firstly, I was going to suggest we take your car anyway because mine was the car that Mikelis saw us in during the surveillance fiasco. Secondly, this afternoon on my way home from the office, I spotted Mikelis standing on the corner. Just as I passed him he took a good look at my car and was staring straight at me. Since we are going into the same neighborhood as the one where he saw us, I do not want to take the chance on him seeing the same goofy women in the same car as the one he saw last night and today. Now, is that clear enough for you?"

Broni actually had the sense to look a little alarmed. Quietly she pulled her car keys out of her purse. "You back out into the street. I will back out also, then you pull into the garage."

She trotted down the driveway to her little garage and unlocked the door. With a mighty heave she sent the door upward where it banged into the end of the track. I backed out and waited for her. Then I pulled into the garage. I opened my driver's door, which promptly banged into the side wall. I pulled it back a little and attempted to squeeze my voluptuous body out through the minimal opening. This garage was built back in the days when the drivers were thinner, the cars were narrower or they kept only one horse. Now I know why Broni leaves her Voluminous Vehicle outside.

I inched sideways down the car, cleaning the entire side with my new raincoat. I hope it's washable. The raincoat, not the car. I finally extracted myself from the form-fitting garage and stepped out into the driveway. I grabbed the bottom of the door and brought it crashing down. Broni had pulled back into the driveway, so I climbed up into the passenger's side. We took off down around the corner toward Laima's house.

"How do we explain my presence?" I asked as we wound our way through the side streets.

"I told her I was bringing a friend."

"That's all, just bringing a friend?"

"That's enough. Sometimes I go visit people with my friends. What is wrong? I think you are getting hypernoid."

"Hypernoid? What is hypernoid?"

"You know, when you think people are out to get you."

"Oh, that clears it up. I think you would be hypernoid too if you had seen Mikelis looking right at you."

"I didn't think he could see us too well last night with the map up over our faces."

"There isn't a map large enough to cover both our heads.

Besides, the second time he saw us there was a large boot-shaped hole right through three counties."

"Ya, you are right. I think we had better be very careful."

"You can say that again." I regretted that the moment I said it.

"Ya, you are ..."

"Never mind," I blurted out. Broni looked insulted. "It's just a figure of speech."

Fortunately we had arrived in front of Laima's house. I recognized it from our adventures of the night before. It was only a short distance from where we first spotted Mikelis last night.

"Are we sure that Mikelis has no reason to know this car?" I asked.

Broni thought for a moment. "No, last night we were too far away and Mikelis left town before I got this car, so he would not have known it was mine. I don't even know if he would remember me. I was mostly just a friend of Aija's."

I followed her up the porch steps of a large two-family house painted a light gray. It seemed like most of the houses in this neighborhood were painted some shade of gray, and the ones that weren't were brown. Broni pushed one of two doorbells beside the front door.

"Does Laima own this house?"

Broni turned and whispered, "Yes, she does. She was able to buy it with the insurance money."

Just as I was about to ask what type of catastrophe had enabled her to buy her own home, the door opened and a slightly past-middle-age lady greeted us with a smile.

"Come in, Broni. This must be your friend Oof. I am very happy to meet you."

"Hello, Laima," Broni said as she stepped through the door.

"It is very nice to meet you, Laima. Broni has spoken of you many times," I said as I shook her hand.

"Thank you. I am honored to have you in my home. Please come in."

We went through another door that led to the living room of the downstairs apartment. It was very pleasantly furnished in a Goodwill sort of way. An overstuffed couch with a slipcover solid with flowers that had bloomed long ago and two puffy chairs with similar textile floral displays. Through the archway I could see a dining room table and a kitchen beyond. It was very homey.

"Oof, may I get you coffee? I have a cinnamon cake also," Laima said.

"That sounds wonderful. Broni told me that you are a very good baker."

"Yes, she is," Broni interjected. "I can remember when I was just a little girl, Laima worked in a bakery and would give me a cookie or a small cake when my mother sent me to get bread."

Perfect place to start asking questions.

"Broni, then you and Laima came from the same town?"

Broni perked up. Darn, she caught on fast.

Laima spoke up. "Yes, my family and Broni's had been there for generations. I knew her mother and grandmother. We all came to this country about the same time."

"So, are there any other people here from the same town?" I asked with great subtlety.

Broni kept quiet. Good thing. It would look too much like a setup if she answered me.

"Yes, there are a few others. I will get the coffee and cake and be right back," Laima said on her way to the kitchen.

I looked around the room. There were some family pictures on a bookcase filled with classic novels. A large picture of a very handsome man dominated the arrangement, with a smaller picture on each side. They were of two young men, who bore quite a resemblance to the man in the middle.

Laima came back from the kitchen with a tray full of goodies. She set it on the coffee table in front of the couch. She poured three cups of coffee from a porcelain coffee pot.

"Laima, that is a beautiful coffee set. Was that in your family?"

"Yes, it belonged to my grandmother. I like to use it when I have company. It is almost the only thing I have of hers."

"It's quite remarkable that it is in such good condition after all these years and making a long trip. Did your grandmother come over here with you?"

"No, she had passed on by then. I came with my husband when our two sons were very little," Laima said as she passed me a cup of coffee and a little plate with a piece of cake.

"Is that them on the bookcase?"

"Yes, that is my husband and two sons."

"They are very handsome. Do they live around here?"

"No. They both graduated from the state university and then had to move away to get good jobs."

She looked rather sad after that. I didn't dare ask about the husband. I didn't see any men's shoes in the front hallway or any other evidence that he was still around.

Broni broke the silence. "Is there any news from anyone since I last talked to you?"

Laima dropped her head and studied her fingernails. Her hands showed that she had not had an easy life. "My niece Aija's husband is back."

Broni feigned surprise. "He is? When did he come back?"

"I think he has been here for about a week." Laima raised her head to look at Broni.

I hoped Broni would remember to ask the right questions and not let Laima know she already knew about Mikelis. I needed to remember to keep my mouth shut, because I wasn't supposed to even know Mikelis.

"Did he come to see Aija and the children?"

Laima said, "No, I talked to her yesterday and she had not seen him. That is a good thing."

She seemed reluctant to say any more. I expect it was because I was there. Broni pushed on.

"If he didn't come back to Aija, why is he here?"

Laima looked back down at her fingernails. "I don't know. I am afraid that he may be doing something that is not good." She looked up at me. "Please forgive us for speaking of this person you do not know. It makes me sad to have to say things about him that are not nice, but I think it is the truth."

I stumbled all over my tongue, trying to protest that it was fine with me if they bad-mouthed this guy. "Laima, please don't apologize. I know you and Broni want to discuss the news in the neighborhood. Go right ahead. I am just sitting here enjoying your delicious cake."

"If he did not go home to Aija, where has he been staying?" Broni asked.

"I think he has been staying with my sister and her husband. They own a tavern just up in the next block and have an apartment upstairs. I talked to my sister a few days ago and she said only that there was someone visiting them from our homeland. I asked who and she said it was better that I didn't know. She was not happy about this person being there. The next day, I saw her husband, Andrievs, who asked me if I knew that Mikelis was visiting."

"Your sister didn't want to talk about it, but your brother-in-law didn't mind?" I said, probably unwisely.

"Oof, he is a good husband to my sister. He provides for her quite well, but sometimes he does things and is with people that are not always good. I think that is why he does not mind that Mikelis is staying there."

"Oh, I see." I decided at this point to keep my mouth shut. Laima was a good, hard-working woman and it was embarrassing to her to have to admit to having borderline criminals in the family. Broni knows her better. I'll let her ask the questions.

"Does your sister's husband know why Mikelis is here?" Broni asked, not very subtly.

"I don't know. I am just afraid for my sister. Mikelis may be up to something and has dragged her husband into it. Andrievs is a good man, but not very smart. In the past he has been tempted to do things that aren't quite right by the promise of money."

Just then the doorbell rang. Laima hesitated, then set her cup down on the tray. She got up and looked out the window. Her face snapped into a stony expression. She opened the apartment door to the vestibule, then opened the outside door.

I could hear her talking and a man answering, but since my command of Livonian is limited to a few curse words that Broni utters from time to time, I couldn't tell what they were saying. Broni's ears perked right up when she heard the man answer. With big eyes she turned to me and whispered, "It is Mikelis."

"Oh," was all I could get out. Laima and her unexpected visitor came into the room.

"Broni, do you remember Mikelis?" Laima said by way of introduction.

"Oh, but yes. It has been several years since I have seen you. How are you?" Broni managed to sound somewhat sincere.

"Mikelis, this is Broni's friend, Oof," Laima continued.

"How do you do? It's nice to meet you." I managed to say this with my head slightly averted to the side, hoping he would not notice what a striking resemblance I bore to one of the lunatics that were following him last night.

"Good evening, ladies. I did not know you had company, Laima. I am here visiting for a few days and I just wanted to see you for a short while."

"Please sit down, Mikelis. We were just discussing some of the people here in the neighborhood that Broni and I know." Laima said, gesturing to the other end of the couch from where I was sitting. I was not too happy about having him sit near me and his ability to see my stunning profile was a little frightening. To counteract the possibility of his recognizing me from the side, since that was what he had seen last night and today, I looked straight at him. I also figured that laughing would be good, because he had seen us in serious moments. So I sat there snapping my head to the left and smiling at everything. I also threw in an occasional tinkly laugh.

Broni started staring at me. I suspect it was because she and Laima had been discussing the death of Laima's aunt to which I reacted like a circus pony, tossing my head and smiling at Mikelis. As soon as I realized this, I calmed down considerably. What I hadn't counted on was the fact that my activity designed to draw attention away from my face, had actually caused Mikelis to stare at me with rapt attention. I don't think Emma Peel would have blown a face-to-face meeting with the enemy with quite such insane abandon.

"Mikelis, do you remember my aunt? She lived just a few houses away with her daughter," Laima said, trying to politely draw him into the conversation. They were still discussing the lady that passed away.

I decided to take the opposite action. I turned away from Mikelis and stared at some pictures on the wall. They seemed to be family portraits. Some of them quite old.

Laima saw me looking at them and remarked, "The second one from the left is my family just before we left home to come here. My mother and father are there and my two sisters and brother. The littlest girl is Aija's mother." Both Broni and Laima looked at Mikelis to see if there would be any response. Even if he was a crook, he had the good sense to put his head down. He must still have some respect for Laima.

I was beginning to think Broni and I should high-tail it out of here. I doubted that Mikelis was going to volunteer details over coffee of whatever he was involved in. Maybe if we left, Laima could find out what he is doing here. Broni must have had about the same thought at about the same time.

Mikelis had just asked Laima for her e-mail address. She laughed and said she didn't have one. In fact, she didn't even own a computer. Broni may not look like it, but sometimes she can think pretty fast on her feet. "Mikelis, I have an e-mail address. If you want to send a message to Laima, send it to me and I will get it to her. I can even send a reply if she wants."

Broni wrote her e-mail address on a business card she pulled out of her pocket and handed it to him. She pulled out another card and asked him for his. He somewhat reluctantly gave it to her as she wrote it down. She stood up and said, "Thank you for the cake and coffee, Laima. It was very nice to see you again. We will go now and give you a chance to visit with Mikelis."

I stood up and said about the same thing, except I added that the cake was very good. We walked over to the door. Laima was right behind us. We turned to her and said goodnight. We were both quiet on the way down the steps until we got into the car.

Then we both started talking at once. "What is he doing there?" Broni spit out.

I added, "I wonder if he is going to tell Laima anything useful. Can you call her tomorrow and find out what he said?"

Broni started the MassiveMobile and we moved forward down the street. "I guess I could. She might wonder why we want to know."

"It isn't like his name hadn't already come up. You can just tell her you're concerned about her brother-in-law getting involved in anything goofy, and that you were worried about her, too. I just hope Mikelis didn't recognize us. I was trying to make my face look different, so he wouldn't."

"Is that why you were shaking your head funny and making odd noises?"

"Those weren't odd noises, that was a tinkly laugh. I thought it would throw him off the trail."

"Oh, I see." We were back in front of Broni's house. I jumped down out of the truck and walked down the driveway to attempt to open her garage door. Broni waited out in the street while I backed my car out and stopped beside her. We both rolled our windows down. "I'll see you in the morning. I have to come in early and do some paperwork on a new listing. Maybe you can talk to Laima tomorrow and see what happened tonight."

"Ok, I will see you. Goodnight." She rolled her window up and turned into her driveway.

I rolled my window up and locked my doors. I guess I was still hypernoid, as Broni would say. I went home and went to bed. This detective stuff tires me out.

15 CHAPTER FIFTEEN

As tired as I was, I didn't sleep very well. I kept waking up with fuzzy pictures in my head. I think my brain was trying to make connections between the people and the facts. Nothing clicked and I just rolled around trying to get back to sleep. Just before dawn, I settled down and got all comfy just as a 25-pound cat jumped up and landed on my stomach. I groaned and rolled over, flopping George down on the blanket on the far side of the bed.

"Go to sleep," I muttered and proceeded to do just that.

I woke up and looked at the clock. 8:45 a.m. I sat up, scattering cats in two directions. I rolled out of bed and headed for the shower. The water raised my consciousness to a semi-vegetative state. By the time I got dressed and performed my ever-hopeful beauty ritual I was nearly awake.

I went down the stairs, followed by George and Ira. We did breakfast. Theirs out of stainless steel bowls on the floor, mine out of a cup while standing at the sink. I grabbed my briefcase and purse and headed out the door. It was nice to have a sunny day that was warm enough to go without a coat. I walked into the office and said hello to Larry at the front desk and Don in his office.

"Hey, Oph, I see you have a new listing. Is it any good?" Don yelled behind me as I tried to escape down the hall.

"It's a real gem, Don. You'll love this one. It's got a full basement and skylights."

I didn't want to tell him what the basement was full of or how the skylights got there. I think both resulted from the big windstorm we had a couple of weeks ago.

"So, have you talked to Laima this morning?"

Broni was busily typing away on her computer. I think she was actually doing office work.

"No, it is too early. I think she has to work tonight, so she tries to sleep later. I will call her about 12 noon."

"Ok, I'm going to go finish my paperwork so I can turn in a new listing."

"Oph. I have a storm in my brain."

"Well, I'm sorry to hear that. Take some aspirin and call me tomorrow."

"Oph, stop being silly. I have an idea in my head. We want to see if Mikelis is connected to Mr. Bosch's bride, yes?"

"No. The answer is no. We have gotten deep enough into this. Let's just let Detective Crowley know if Laima found out anything and then we can rest easy without putting ourselves in danger, like we have probably already done."

"Now I will tell you my plan."

I just groaned and sat down.

"I have been looking on the Internet this morning for mail-order brides."

"Broni, I didn't know you were in the market for one."

She gave me a disgusted look and continued.

"I have found several Web sites that have them. I also found out that they are not illegal, but the person trying to get one has to get a fiancée visa for them to get into this country. I wonder if Mr. Bosch knows this?"

"How do you get this visa?" I asked

"It says the man has to have met the girl first and then apply for the visa. He can pay for her expenses. They have to get married within ninety days of her arrival here. They also have to prove a fiancée relationship."

I didn't even want to think about the questions on that last form.

"Broni, how could Mr. Bosch have already met this girl?"

"I don't know. I don't think he has been out of town long enough to go to Latvia, get to know a young lady and come back. That is one of the requirements."

"Are there any exceptions to that rule?"

Broni started studying the screen again. She scrolled through several pages before she exclaimed, "Yes, there is an exception if it is not customary for the bride and groom to meet before the wedding or if the meeting would create undue hardship."

"Is it customary to meet the groom before the wedding in your village?"

"Yes, of course it is. We don't have arranged marriages."

"Then that exception doesn't apply in this case, does it?" I just had a horrible thought. "Broni, what if Mr. Bosch doesn't even know about all this? What if Mikelis is telling him that she can just come over here? Maybe he doesn't know about all the paperwork and having to meet the girl and actually being engaged before she can get into the country."

Broni was still reading. "There are a lot of forms to fill out and it costs quite a bit, too. Plus he has to pay her expenses to get here and sign a form saying that he will provide financial support."

"That isn't a problem; I think Mr. Bosch has a very successful business. I would suspect that he is also rather frugal and invests his money safely. But what if he doesn't know about all the red tape? Could he have trusted Mikelis to arrange everything for him?"

"That could be it, Oph. If Mikelis is involved with the mail-order bride, he may have just told Mr. Bosch that he would take care of everything in exchange for a fee. Probably a very high fee."

"This may be worse than we thought. Mr. Bosch may be involved in a giant bride scam."

She gave me strange look and said, "Oph, I think the brides are normal sized."

"What? Oh no, I meant a giant scam, not a giant bride. Oh, never mind." I started to leave the room.

"Wait, Oph, you haven't heard my idea."

I was hoping she had forgotten about that. "Ok, what is it?"

"On most of the Web sites there is a place to sign up to be a mail-order bride. I searched for a Web site that promised girls from Latvia. Then I looked through the e-mail addresses that were given for contacting them. I found an address that matched the one that Mikelis wrote down last night!"

I began to get a slightly queasy feeling in my stomach. I was afraid what I was going to hear next.

"So, Oph, what I can do is apply to be a mail-order bride on Mikelis' Web site and see what happens!"

I was afraid of this.

"Broni. I am not even sure how to go about telling you how nuts you are. I have been rendered semi-speechless at the sheer idiocy of your plan. How can this possibly work and what is it that you are going to prove?"

"It is easy. Perhaps you could be rendered totally speechless so I could explain."

I think that was an attempt at humor. Anyway, I will be quiet and try to make some sense out of whatever she says.

"Thank you, Oph. Now, I will send him an application and tell him I am visiting in the United States but I will be home next week and can meet with him. That gives me a week to correspond with him and find out things."

"So, what happens when he says he is also in the United States and can meet with you right away?"

She looked thoughtful. Maybe that had not occurred to her in the intricate planning that took place whilst hatching this scatterbrained plot.

"Maybe he will want to wait until he gets home."

"And maybe he won't. And don't forget, he has seen both of us. He would recognize you." And, I didn't add, maybe not all of the mail-order brides were over 6 feet tall and built like a sequoia.

"I am not really going to meet with him. They want a picture, so I found this one in a magazine." She held up a clipping that looked like it was from an old Life magazine. A very old one. It was the famous cover shot of Marilyn Monroe that appeared on the cover of Life in 1952.

"Broni, where did you get this?"

"There were a pile of old magazines in my garage when I bought my house. This is the cover of one of them. Why? What is wrong with it?"

"For one thing, it is a very famous photograph of a very famous person. If anyone in the U.S. saw this picture, they would immediately know who it was. Secondly, if you had not destroyed the magazine, it would be worth some money. Don't tear up any more of those magazines until we look them up on an online auction site. Are you beginning to see the pitfalls in this plan?"

"I will find a different picture."

"That's a start. Now it's almost noon. Call Laima and see if she found out anything last night. I am going back to my office to finish my paperwork and in the meantime, do not try to sell yourself on the Internet."

I could feel her eyes boring into my back as I left her office. I had been working at my desk for only a few minutes when Broni came bounding down the hall and filled my doorway.

"Laima says that Mikelis is here with another man from home. He told her that he was here on business but seemed to be rather nervous about it. She asked what kind of business. He just said it involved quite a bit of money and didn't say anything more. She said he acted a little odd. He did ask her how Aija and the girls were. She wondered if that was why he came to see her. She thought that was odd, too, since he was the one that left them. That's about all."

"It's interesting that there is another man here with him. Why would he need somebody else? If he is here promoting his bride-peddling business, I should think he could do it alone."

"I do not know that, but perhaps if I were to contact him by e-mail, and offer to be a bride, I could find out these things," she said breathlessly.

"You really want to do this, don't you? Even after Detective Crowley told us to lay off, you still think you should go ahead."

"Yes, I do," she stated belligerently.

"Let's maybe do something less dangerous. How about talking to Mr. Bosch again? He seems harmless."

Broni looked thoughtful. "I think my plan is better. Mr. Bosch did not want to talk about the bride when we asked him last time. He is probably afraid of us now that you dragged him through the door."

"I didn't exactly drag him." Broni gave me a look that indicated she didn't agree.

"Oph, we have to find out what's going on. I will be very careful. I will tell him I cannot meet with him until I get home to Latvia. It will work. At least we will get some more information."

I realized there was no use trying to dissuade her. Standing in her way would be futile at best, and dangerous at worst.

"Broni, don't you think we should tell the police? I'll call Detective Crowley for you."

"No, I do not think that would be a good idea. I will just get started on my e-mail message now." She backed out of my office and trotted back to hers. I guess we are on our way to confronting Mikelis. Maybe I should sign up to be a mail-order bride, too. Being the regular kind hadn't worked out very well. He could hardly resist two such ravishing beauties.

"Oph." Broni was back in my doorway. "I think you should be a mail-order bride too. We can find a picture for you to use."

Oh, good. I can just see it now. Eleanor Roosevelt in a swimsuit. "Uh, maybe we should just try one at a time."

"Ok. I will go write my e-mail."

Just about then I heard the front door open. I looked up as Detective Bert Crowley passed my office door. I jumped up from my chair and dashed after the semi-handsome police officer. "Detective Crowley, how nice to see you." He stopped in his tracks about halfway down the hall.

"Is there something we can do for you?"

"Hello, Ms. Olsen. I was just wondering what you could tell me today." I think there was a slightly sarcastic tone to his voice.

"I don't know if I can help you, but why don't you come into my office and have a seat." I led the way into the office and closed the door. I gestured for him to sit in the chair in front of my desk. I sat down behind the desk, hoping he would notice the grace and coordination with which I performed that action.

"How is the investigation going?" I said, batting my eyelashes just a tiny bit. I didn't want to be brazen.

"It's coming along. I just wanted to find out if either of you ladies had any information that you might like to share with me."

"Information? I'm afraid we don't have anything. We talked to you just the other day and we took your warning to heart about not interfering."

"Ms. Olsen. You are aware of the fact that we have been following a Latvian national with the first name of Mikelis. Does that ring any bells in your noggin? It should, considering we just had this conversation and he was seen entering a house last evening that you and your tall sidekick had also entered."

"Uh, I seem to recall that conversation."

"Yes, that's right. Now are you going to tell me the rest of the story?" He looked right into my big blue eyes. I was hoping they would have some effect on him. That did not appear to be the case.

"Rest of the story? Oh, you mean how we may have run into him last night?"

"Yes, that story."

"Well, it was an accident. Broni asked me to go with her to visit a friend of hers. The friend happens to be the aunt of Mikelis' wife, Aija. As we were talking to Laima, the doorbell rang, and lo and behold, it was Mikelis. He came in, sat down and visited for a few minutes, then we left. That's about it." I treated him to one of my most alluring smiles.

"And you did not recruit Laima to pump Mikelis for more info? And you did not check with her this morning to see what she found out? Come on, Ms. Olsen, don't let me down. I know you are more resourceful than that." He leaned back in the chair and unleashed the full power of his 12-watt smile directly at me.

"Detective Crowley. Thank you for the compliment. At least I think that's what it was. And I guess it's silly of us to try to fool such an expert detective as you." Hoo, boy the fertilizer was flying thick and fast. "Yes, we did question Laima about Mikelis. All she could tell us was that her brother-in-law that owns the little tavern in the next block told her Mikelis was visiting. He didn't say why he was here. Laima was suspicious because the brother-in-law seems to have a tendency to get involved in things that make money, but are not completely aboveboard, if you get my drift. And yes, you are also correct about talking to her this morning. Broni called her and found out that Mikelis is here with another man from home and he asked about his wife and children. That's it. She couldn't tell us anything more. That's the whole story."

Ok, maybe not the whole story. I debated telling him the rest, like the fact that Broni was, at this very moment, trying to sell her body on the Internet. In a way, I wanted to tell him, but Broni would probably do physical harm to my person if he stopped her in the middle of her becoming a mail-order bride. On the other hand, it may already be too late. It only takes a moment to send an e-mail and maybe she saw him coming and sent it real fast before he could stop her. Detective Crowley was staring at me. I presumed it was due to my spellbinding, overwhelming beauty. That was not to be. Apparently my internal ponderings had resulted in a real-time gap in conversation. He was more likely staring at me because he wondered why I had a goofy expression on my face.

"Ms. Olsen, are you sure that's the whole story? You seem to be engaged in deep rumination."

"I do? Oh, forgive me. I have a tendency to drift off during moments of deep rumination. Are you aware of the fact that rumination can mean thinking about things, nearly to the point of obsession and that it also refers to the eating habits of a ruminant which involves bringing one's partially digested stomach contents back up to enjoy it a second time? I am hardly flattered by your claim that I am in rumination. By the way, if we are going to be seeing one another fairly frequently, perhaps you should call me Ophelia."

"Ophelia, I most certainly did not mean to compare you to one of our bovine friends. I was merely remarking that you were in a contemplative state."

I have found the perfect man. Not too bald, steady job and he talks just like me. And did I detect a glimmer of desire in those big dark eyes?

"I'm sure you meant no insult, Detective. Not that I am insulted by the thought of comparison to the majestic bovine family, it's just that in the vernacular of the common folk, to be compared to a cow is generally not considered a compliment."

"A point well taken, Ophelia. I think it would expedite our communication if you would call me Bert."

"Bert. Thank you. I would consider it an honor."

Why the hell do we both sound like a bad Katharine Hepburn movie? I know my mind works in mysterious ways, but to find a kindred spirit in the police department? I talk like this when I am nervous. I wonder if he has the same problem?

"Ophelia, I need to emphasize again that there are multiple investigations continuing in the death of the Latvian gentleman and the possible connection of Mikelis to this crime. I would be most distressed if you or your sidekick were to be endangering yourselves in your pursuit of a solution. I can assure you that we are doing everything possible to bring this to a successful conclusion. I appreciate the information you have been able to obtain, but we are progressing quite well and I think it would be in your best interests to step back from the persons of interest in this case. Mikelis saw both of you last night. Depending on his level of involvement in any criminal activities, it could be very dangerous for you to be seen by him again. Especially if you appear to be tailing him. So far I have suggested somewhat strongly that you steer clear of anyone with any possible ties to the case. I now have to insist that you do not do any more snooping around." As he talked, he sat forward in his chair and as he finished his lecture, his hand covered mine and stayed there.

Unaccustomed as I am to gentlemen taking my hand, I'm afraid I drew a breath a little sharply. I hope he didn't notice. I didn't mind the present situation at all. Unfortunately, before he could express his undying passion for me, which I'm sure he was on the verge of, my office door flew open and Broni appeared. She took in the scene rapidly and was staring at our joined hands on the desk. I quickly pulled my hand back.

"So, Broni, Detective Crowley came to visit. I told him about our running into Mikelis last night."

"Oh, hello, Detective. How are you today?"

Bert, as I shall now refer to him, stood up and turned to Broni. "Good afternoon, Ms. Z. I was just explaining to Ms. Olsen that I am grateful for the information you have supplied, but I need the two of you to be very diligent about avoiding any further contact with Mikelis, or anyone associated with him. This is in the interest of your personal safety."

"Oh, yes, sir. We will be very careful."

Bert gave her a wary glance. "I need to get back to the station. Good afternoon, ladies."

He gave me a slight backward glance as he left my office and walked out the front door. Broni was staring at me. I asked, "So, what's new in your office?"

"What is new in my office? What is new in your office? I stumble upon you and the detective holding hands? It is a good thing I got here when I did. He may have tried to put moves on you."

"Broni, the detective was just being nice. He had just given me a lecture on staying away from the bad guys, whoever they may be. Mikelis probably being one of them. That's all."

I sincerely hoped I was wrong, that that wasn't all it was.

"Oph, you cannot fool me. I saw the two of you making reindeer eyes at each other. It was not to be mistaken for a mere friendly gesture. Are you becoming interested in the detective?"

"He seems like a nice guy. That's all. Now, what have you been doing back there? Did you get any offers over five dollars yet?"

She looked insulted. "That is not how it works. The Web site said to send an e-mail if I was interested in meeting men from the United States. So, I sent an e-mail."

"What did you tell them in the e-mail?" I asked, not really wanting to know the answer.

"The instructions said to tell them about myself. So I did. I told them I was five feet, four inches tall. I told them I had blonde hair that was long. I also have blue eyes and good measurements."

"Good measurements? What are good ones? I don't think any of the measurements you or I have are considered good ones. Most of those girls probably fib a little in their initial contact. And taking a foot off your height is probably just a little fib," I said, more to myself than anyone.

Broni wasn't really paying attention to me anyway. I think she was caught up in the glamour of being an international mail-order beauty. She turned to go out the door.

"I must to back to my desk and see if I have an answer yet." She floated down the hallway.

Now we've done it. Made direct contact with a possible bad guy. Heretofore, we had just been running around on the fringes of whatever is going on. I think we need to formulate a plan to handle any response on Mikelis' part. I don't believe any serious thought has been given to this as yet. I wanted to look at Broni's e-mail to see what else she told him beside the somewhat fictitious physical attributes.

Broni was typing when I reached her desk.

"Ok, what exactly was in that e-mail? I think I should see it because we need to decide what to do when Mikelis does contact you. And what are you writing now?" I asked, hoping she wasn't sending more messages right away.

"I am just composing a series of additional notes that I may use in the future. I shall save them and have them ready. Here is the first e-mail."

I read the message. It wasn't too bad. She didn't tell him where she was in the U.S. That was good. I provoked a nasty look from her when I chuckled at her physical description.

"That's good. Let's wait and see what he says. Don't answer him without letting me see it first. Ok? We need to be really careful about this. I promised Bert, er, Detective Crowley that we would not get involved any more."

Broni looked up, "Bert? The detective is now Bert? The holding hands was just being friendly? I think you had better watch out."

I should be so lucky. "Don't worry. I'm sure his intentions are merely to make friends with us so he can find out what we know. He certainly has no interest in me over and above this case."

"Well, maybe so, but there is an old saying that my grandmother told me. 'In the fall, when the antlers have grown once again, the reindeer go looking for mates.'"

"It's spring and I haven't noticed any antlers on the detective. I'm going to go get my paperwork done with hopefully no more interruptions. Let me know if you get any messages."

I went back to my office again, befuddled by the wisdom of Broni's grandmother. I finished the listing and took it back to Broni.

"Can you get this in the system today or are we too busy becoming a cyber-slut?"

"That is not funny, Oph. We are doing important work here. This could help the police."

"And don't forget the Latvian government. They are in this, too."

"I will get your listing in the system now. I have not heard from the e-mail."

"You know, this may not work. If Mikelis is here, he may not have access to a computer to check his e-mail. And the other guy with him may be the only other participant in this whole scheme. I doubt they have an office staff back in the old country taking orders for brides. It may be a long time before he ever sees your message."

"We don't know. Maybe he has many people working for

him."

"You're right. We don't know much about him. I have to make some phone calls."

I went back to my office, trying to piece together what we did know and it wasn't much. The more we found out, the more convoluted it became.

We know that Mikelis and Bosch know each other and that Bosch is expecting a bride from far away. Mikelis is connected with obtaining these brides, we assume. That is circumstantial evidence. The dead guy was Latvian. Another piece of circumstantial evidence that he is connected to all this, too. So, is Mikelis a murderer? Possibly. What about the other guy with him? Either one or both could be the murderer. Selling mail-order brides doesn't seem like a business that would be lucrative enough to murder anyone. Some of this doesn't quite make sense.

I have to call Mr. Fitch about his house. John, the agent who showed the Fitch house on Southampton last week with his clients Ralphie and Miss Goldfritz, called me this morning to say he has an offer on the property. I need to find a time when Mr. Fitch and Mother are available to sit down and have the offer presented to them.

He answered on the third ring. "Mr. Fitch? It's Ophelia Olsen. How are you today?"

"I'm very well, Miss Olsen, and you?"

"I'm fine, thank you. I have good news. Do remember the people that came through the house a few days ago, Mr. Spadafora and Miss Goldfritz?"

"Yes, I think so. Blonde and pink, if I remember."

I had to chuckle, Alfred was observant and had a sense of humor. "Yes, that's about right. Well, their agent called me and says they have an offer for you to look at. I need to find out when you would be available."

"Well, I believe anytime later today would be fine. Other

than right at dinner time. I have to take Mother to the club. We would be gone from about 5 until about 7. Would 7:30 be good for you?"

"I will check with the other agent and call you back, but that sounds good to me. I'll call you as soon as I hear from him."

"That's fine, Miss Olsen. I will be here until about 5. Thank you."

We bid each other goodbye and I immediately called John. I got him right away and agreed to meet at the Fitches' house at 7:30. I called Mr. Fitch back, gave him the news and said I'd see them later.

Where did the time go? It was almost 3:30. I guess being involved in international intrigue was very time-consuming. I always noticed that Emma Peel and John Steed never seemed to have much extra time on their hands. At that point the door opened and in walked the semi-handsome partial hunk, Detective Bert Crowley.

"Good afternoon, Ophelia."

"Hello, Bert. Didn't I just see you this morning?"

"Indeed you did. I wanted to stop and give you some news. I don't believe I ever told you about the medical examiner's report on the body you found."

"When you were here that day, you said it looked like some kind of whack on the head."

"That was just idle conjecture at that point, but the ME's office said it was definitely a very hard blow to the top of his head with probably a heavy object. The damage to the top of his skull led them to that conclusion."

"Then I guess that lets out any other causes like poisoned darts or culture shock."

"It does. So, if we are looking for a killer, our suspicion of Mikelis doesn't add up. He has an artificial hand and is not very tall. Have you run across anyone in your travels that fits the description?"

I thought for a moment. "Only Broni."

He looked at me very seriously. "She said she didn't know the man."

"I'm kidding. Broni would never hurt anyone. She is opposed to any kind of violence. She won't even squash spiders. She gives them a lecture and throws them outdoors."

Bert smiled. "Ok, you got me. I presume you didn't run into anyone else that fits the description."

"No, but maybe you'd better ask Broni if there's anyone she knows like that."

"I will. I have to get back to my office. It was nice to see you again. I'll be in touch."

"Bye, Bert," I said, using the sultry Emma Peel tone. I waved about two minutes later as he passed my office on his way out after interrogating Broni.

I thought it was about time to go home and do a little work there.

"Broni. I'm leaving," I yelled down the hallway.

"Wait a minute." She came galumphing out of her office. "Did the detective tell you about the dead man or were you too busy holding hands?" She laughed.

"Very funny. Yes he did tell me that it was a heavy object and that they are presuming it was someone tall and strong. Did he ask you if you knew anyone like that? I told him the only person I knew like that was you."

"That is also very funny. I would not do that. I don't know anybody that fits that description."

"Broni, I was kidding and he knew it. I am going to go home. I've got work I should do there and it will soon be supper time for the Gershwin brothers."

"Ok. Are you coming in tomorrow?"

"Of course, I wouldn't miss it for the world. One never knows what excitement may pop up. Beside, I have to go to the Fitches' house on Southampton tonight. Another agent is presenting an offer. Hopefully I will have paperwork for you in the morning. " I gathered up my bag and purse. "See you tomorrow."

"Bye."

I started out the door and a thought popped into my head. I turned and yelled at Broni's back as she went down the hallway. "If you get any response from your flesh-peddling e-mail, you call me immediately, ok?" It occurred to me she might just conveniently forget to tell me about a message from Mikelis. It might seem more exciting to handle it on her own.

She hesitated and yelled back, "Ok."

I went on out the door and threw my stuff into the back seat of my car. I took a look at the side of it. A few scratches here and there and a profile that definitely didn't match the baby blue Lotus that belonged to Emma Peel. That's probably just as well. I thought about this as I drove home. Emma must have a stronger constitution than I do. I don't think I could be around bad guys to the extent that she is. My dream of driving into a secluded cave is pretty well shot, too. Home to my plain white garage door.

Same routine, different night. Work on the yard a little, feed the boys and eat whatever fell out when I opened the refrigerator door. Tonight the same routine seemed good. It was comfortable and free of excitement. It was free of criminals and dead guys. I think I'll be a professional hermit. I wonder how they get paid? Perhaps some research would be in order before I commit myself to that career track. This decision needed to be put aside for the time being. I had to be at the Fitches' house in half an hour.

I completed my beauty ritual in record time. Actually it was plenty of time to spend on such futile gestures.

I arrived at the Fitch house right on time. I parked on the street and went to the front door. Alfred answered on the first ring of the doorbell.

"Good evening, Miss Olsen. How nice to see you."

Sure, nice to see me now that you know an offer is coming in. "Good evening, Mr. Fitch. You're looking very well."

"Thank you. Please come in."

I stepped into the foyer. "Mr. Fitch, how is your mother this evening?"

He smiled. "Don't be afraid, Miss Olsen. She isn't any more disagreeable than usual."

I laughed and he continued, "I think she will be cooperative, as long as everything is explained to her."

"Don't worry. As soon as we see the contract I will explain it all."

"Excellent, Miss Olsen, I have every confidence in you. Where do you think we should gather?"

As we walked across the foyer through the living room I suggested the dining room. "I think that would be the best. We can spread the papers out to look at them."

"The dining room it is. Please have a seat wherever you would like. I will go get Mother. She is upstairs freshening up. I'll be back shortly."

Freshening up? I wonder what that entails. Probably a powder puff covered with cinnamon to pat on the dried apple cheeks. Perhaps a moth ball or two under the arms.

I got my yellow legal pad and my calculator out of my bag and set them on the table. There were a couple of beautiful paintings on the walls. I strolled around the table to get a better look. I recognized the signatures. Very impressive. I wonder if this stuff will be sold locally? Probably not. If Mother can't take them with her I suspect they'll be sent to New York to an auction house.

I heard a peculiar whirring sound. Alfred must be bringing her down on the service elevator between the kitchen and garage.

I could hear her voice even before the door from the kitchen opened. In a moment it did and Mrs. Fitch came tottering through the door followed by Alfred holding her elbow.

"Olsen. What's this all about? Those trailer park people are coming here tonight?"

"Good evening, Mrs. Fitch. No, the potential buyers won't be here. Their agent will be bringing us an offer to consider. I'd like to talk to you for a couple of minutes before he arrives."

"By all means, Miss Olsen. Here, Mother, why don't you sit next to Miss Olsen. That way she can show you the papers and explain them," Alfred said as he seated her on my right. Alfred took a seat at the end of the table to my left.

"John, the agent who brought Mr. Spadafora and Miss Goldfritz through your house, will be bringing the contract. He will present it to us. That means he will tell us about his buyers, and then tell us the terms of the contract, including the price that they are offering. After he does this, we will ask him any questions about the terms that may not be clear. Then we ask him to leave the room while we discuss the contract. If the price and terms are acceptable to you, both of you will then sign the contract and the deal is done. If there is anything to which you object, we will tell John and he will contact his buyers to see if they will change the item. The only important thing to remember is that we just let him present the offer and we don't discuss the terms and price until he has left the room." I sat back hoping I had Mother's cooperation.

Just at that point the doorbell rang. Alfred stood up. "I'll get the door."

Mother just sat in her chair, glowering at me. It was more than a little frightening because she was sitting so close to me. Distance makes a look like that less scary.

Alfred entered the dining room with John in tow.

"Good evening, John. Do you remember Mrs. Fitch?" I ventured.

"Yes. Hello. Nice to see you again." John was visibly cowed

at the sight of Mother Fitch, who had changed her target from me to him.

"John, why don't you sit here on the end of the table." I pointed to the big armchair at the foot of the table.

"Thank you, Ophelia."

John sat down and got out four copies of the contract. He started explaining the terms, how the buyers were going to pay for the house, the fact that they did want a home inspection and finally the price.

Mother Fitch stared at him the entire time. Talk about psyching somebody out.

"Thank you, John. Mr. or Mrs. Fitch, do either of you have any questions about anything John has said?"

"No, I don't. You made it quite clear, John. Mother, do you have any questions?" Alfred said.

The little mouth started churning and grinding like somebody had put coffee beans in it and set it on "coarse."

"No, let's get on with it. I want to talk to Olsen," finally came out of the hole in the middle of the dried apple.

"Thank you, John. Let me show you to the living room. You can have a seat there while we discuss your offer."

I led John into the living room and suggested he sit in the club chair on the far wall that adjoined the library. That way he was far enough away to not be able to hear our conversation. I had no idea what this discussion would be like. I returned to the dining room and sat down.

"Mrs. and Mr. Fitch. Let's go through this contract. I want to explain everything in it and what ramifications the terms have for you."

I started on page one and went through the entire thirteen pages, the riders and the addendum stating that the buyers would like Mrs. Fitch's bed.

Things were going good until we got to that part. The mere mention of Miss Goldfritz having the bed set forth a veritable storm of twitching.

"Do you mean that hooker is going to use my bed for heaven only knows what?"

I didn't want to mention that we probably all knew what.

""Mrs. Fitch, they are asking that the bed be included in the sale. This is not too unusual. It is one of the terms that we can agree to or not."

The face began to twist and bend. The mouth opened and out came a surprisingly lucid and clear sentence. "That bed has been in my family for four generations. It is not staying here for that Blond Bimbo to hop around on."

Alfred put his head down and contemplated the tabletop. I was hoping John couldn't hear the names being applied to his client.

"Let's talk about the rest of the contract," I said. "They are paying cash for the house. So we don't have to worry about their ability to get a mortgage, also we do not have to have a bank appraiser come in to look at anything. They are willing to accept the house in its present condition. They do want a home inspection, but that is just for their information."

Mother piped up again. "What about the price? Let's squeeze some more money out of them. That old fool she was with looks like he's got it."

"Mrs. Fitch. The house was on the market for two hundred and seventy-nine thousand dollars. They have offered you two hundred seventy-five cash. That is an extremely good offer. We could counter at a higher price, but we may lose them. I suggest we accept the price and the home inspection and tell them we do not accept the inclusion of the bed. How does that sound?"

Alfred spoke for the first time since we started. "Miss Olsen. I think the contract is quite good as you explained it. We will accept your judgment on the price and as you pointed out, having cash is very good. Mother is quite adamant about the bed, so we will not accept that condition. Do you see any potential problems with this offer?"

"Mr. Fitch, the only uncertainty we have is the home inspector's report. Some buyers have gotten the idea that any little thing the inspector finds has to be repaired by the seller. That is not the purpose of it, but if they should ask you to repair anything, I think we should just consider those items when or if they come up. There may be minor things that would be worth your while to have repaired just to keep them happy."

Mother started bouncing a little in her chair. Either she had gas or was getting ready to say something. Finally she bounced out a couple of sentences. "Olsen, I'm not fixing anything. They can take it or leave it."

Alfred looked mildly amused. "Miss Olsen, let's tell the gentleman we'll take it."

I got up and went to the dining room door. I opened it and called, "John, will you come back now, please?"

After we were all seated in the dining room again, I spoke. "John, Mrs. and Mr. Fitch have agreed to the price and the conditions with the exception of the addendum asking for the bed. That particular piece of furniture has been in Mrs. Fitch's family for several generations and is a family heirloom. I'm sure your clients will understand why we have to eliminate that request."

"I will call them and find out if that's acceptable to them. I'll be right back." He went into the living room to use his cell phone.

While he was out making his call, Mrs. Fitch turned to Alfred. "Now what? We have to find somewhere to live. And don't get any bright ideas about sticking me in one of those homes where they make you string beads all day. Olsen, I told you to find me a condo with a good-looking door man."

"I promise, if we get this contract all signed, I'll start looking first thing in the morning." I don't think "good-looking doormen" is a valid search criteria in the system. I may have to research this myself. In person.

John came back into the room. "They have discussed it and have agreed to forget the bed."

"Good, then let me get some pens out and we'll get this signed." I got two more pens out of my bag and handed one to Alfred and one to Mother. I showed them all the places they had to sign and we accomplished this in relative silence.

When we were all done I handed John his two copies. "Thank you, John, for bringing us this offer. I'm sure your clients will be very happy here.

"Thank you, Ophelia, and thank you, Mr. and Mrs. Fitch. I will tell my clients they have a new home. Good night." I walked him to the front door.

"Thanks again, John."

"No problem, Ophelia. Good luck."

I shut the door behind him and went back to the table.

"Congratulations, Mrs. Fitch. Your house is sold."

"Don't remind me, Olsen. Now I have to figure out what to do with all this stuff and you have to find me a hot doorman."

I laughed. "I'll start looking first thing in the morning. Do you think I should go around and inspect the doormen myself?

Mother Fitch let out a cackle. "I'll bet you'd like that, wouldn't you, Olsen? Are you married?"

Alfred put his head down again. "Mother, I'm not sure that's an appropriate question for Miss Olsen."

"Oh, loosen up, Alfred. You used to be more fun."

"No, Mrs. Fitch, I'm not married right now."

"Right now? Were you?"

"Yes, at one time."

"Then get out there and find two good-looking doormen." She cackled. Alfred looked appalled.

For a cackle, it was infectious. All of us started to laugh, even Alfred.

"I'll do that, Mrs. Fitch. Here is your copy of the contract. Remember, the buyers are asking for a closing to take place in about two months. We need to start looking at condos as soon as possible. I will call you tomorrow and let you know what's available. I think you mentioned the ones over by the river, right?"

Alfred spoke. "Miss Olsen. We will need two condos, side by side. We can then have alterations done if necessary to connect them. Mother will need at least two bedrooms, three if possible, and I would like two bedrooms."

Mother Fitch was scowling at this. "You still have that goofy idea that I'm going to need a live-in nursemaid, don't you?"

"Not right away, but I think we should plan for the future. Someday you'll be older and may need a little help."

"Tomorrow I'll be older, you jerk, and I suppose you're right." She cackled again.

"Well, we are done with our paperwork, so I will run along and let you get to bed. I'll talk to you in the morning as soon as I find some condos for us to look at."

Mother Fitch swiveled her wizened-up little face toward Alfred. "Are you going to be home in the morning? I thought you told me you had a meeting."

"Oh, yes, that's right. I have to be at a meeting at eight and probably won't be done until around 10:30. I should be home by eleven," Alfred volunteered.

"Would you prefer I called after you got home?"

"Yes, that would be a good idea."

Mother piped up again. "Is this meeting with those guys you used to work for?"

Alfred looked like he didn't want to answer that question. "Just some people I knew."

"Are you investigating somebody again?"

"No, Mother. I'm not. Miss Olsen, it was nice to see you and we thank you for all your hard work in selling our house. I will look forward to talking to you tomorrow and finding our new home."

Being no dummy, I took the hint and stood up. "I'm just glad we were able to sell it so quickly. I'll talk to you tomorrow. Good night, Mrs. Fitch."

"Good night, Olsen. I'm going to bed now, Alfred." Alfred started to help her up. "Leave me alone. I can get from here to the elevator. I have to start getting more limber if I'm going to chase that doorman." She cackled as she shuffled off toward the kitchen.

Alfred Fitch walked me to the front door. "Miss Olsen. Thank you again. I also thank you for being kind to Mother. She can be a little trying at times."

"Mr. Fitch. I think your mother is kind of cute in a strange way. Good night."

I could hear him chuckling as he closed the door behind me. Alfred was a very nice-looking man. About twenty years ago, he would have been a real knockout. I guessed he was about twenty years older than I was. For his age, he appeared to be in excellent condition. I wondered if he worked out. Oh, well. I guess it doesn't make much difference. He didn't appear to be married, probably a widower. Or maybe never married. Or maybe I'd just better keep my mind on my business.

When I got home, I got on the computer to check my e-mail. Nothing from Broni. I opened another browser window and searched for Latvian brides. I got a lot of possibilities. Most of which promised females for all kinds of purposes, not necessarily involving becoming a bride. I knew the Internet had a lot of disgusting stuff on it, but this was my first experience at actually running across much of it. I finally found what looked to be Mikelis' Web site. At least I think it was, judging by my faint remembrance of the e-mail address that he gave Broni. This is interesting. All the pictures of the girls looked very professional. I wonder what we are going to be able to find to send in for Broni's picture that will be as good as these. It certainly can't be a real, live, unretouched photo of her, unless we find somebody willing to spend about four hours with an airbrush. It is very curious that every girl that applies to be a mail-order bride has these glamorous pictures. Is it possible that every little village in Latvia has a photographer's studio and every girl has the money to spend there? It is also curious that there isn't one ugly face. I'll have to talk to Broni about this. Maybe this is why she left.

I wound up my evening by practicing putting golf balls into my little plastic ball return machine. When the ball goes into the opening a gopher pops up and yells, "nice shot" or a couple of other inanities, apparently depending on its mood. It should yell when I miss the hole. I guess that motivational approach didn't occur to the manufacturer. Or the gopher, for that matter. The gopher also causes George and Ira to high-tail it out of the room and peek around the corner.

16 CHAPTER SIXTEEN

The garage door was still white. Good thing. I have totally lost my desire to follow in Emma's footsteps. I'll use that bucket of epoxy I bought to glue the bushes on the garage door for something else.

I pulled into the office parking lot and parked beside the Broni-mobile. There were a few other cars here. Must be some of the agents are meeting clients this morning. I went in and put my stuff down on my desk. The office was buzzing with activity. Don the office manager was flitting from office to office smacking his lips as he observed agents meeting with clients and writing contracts.

"Hey, Oph. How're you doing?" Don yelled.

"Fine, Don," I yelled back, even though we were only five feet apart.

"Had any offers on that Southampton house yet?"

"Yes, in fact I sold it last night. I am going to finish up the paper work this morning and turn in the contracts and the report of sale."

He practically twirled in the air. "Oh, very good. How much did you get for it?"

"We didn't do too badly. Two seventy-five cash."

"Nice work, Oph. You might be agent of the month!"

"Don't hold your breath, Don. I don't have much of a chance

with old Natalie out there peddling her wares."

Don cringed a little at my description of Natalie Krakowski, the office princess. Also, he secretly lusted after her bleached blonde, gold-chained, war-painted charm. At least he thought it was secret, but unfortunately for him, everybody knew about it.

"It's only the fourth of the month. I would need several more sales of that size to get ahead of Natalie." I would also need a couple of other things the same size as Natalie's. I don't find it a rewarding goal. Her tactics leave a little to be desired in the ethics department. I guess love is blind. Don didn't seem to see it that way.

"She is usually our top salesman," Don said.

"She usually is, that's for sure," I uttered inanely. I think he meant top-heavy. He also left out the part about him directing most of the incoming leads to Natalie. Where she was concerned, he didn't do his thinking with his brain, if you get my drift. Don's wife had run off with somebody more interesting a couple of years ago. I think it was the guy that drove the poultry truck.

I wandered toward my office in an attempt to cut this scintillating conversation short. Fortunately for me, Larry came through the door and Don pounced on him, demanding to know what he had sold this morning.

I sat down at my desk and started my paperwork. I thought about the Fitches while I worked. Mother's bark was worse than her bite. She had a sense of humor. Alfred was interesting. He appeared to be very intelligent. I wondered what he did for a living. I know his mother has lived in that house for years, but I don't remember hearing that her son lived there. Maybe he moved back home after retirement. Her husband died about fifteen years ago, I thought I remembered reading in the paper. He was the president of the iron foundry that was started by Mrs. Fitch's father. I wondered why Mother asked Alfred if he was investigating anything. Maybe he could help us with the bride thing. My mind is wandering again. I have to get this paperwork done.

The daylight reaching my office from the front window was suddenly diminished by Broni appearing in my doorway. "Don said you sold Southampton last night. Do you have your contracts and report ready to go?"

"I'm working on it. Why are you in such a rush?

"Because I want to get all the work done in case I get a message back from Mikelis."

"Are you going to run out the door and meet him instantly?"

"No, of course not, but I want to be able to concentrate."

"Ok, then let me finish this. I'll bring it to you in a couple of minutes."

"All right, but hurry."

She scurried back to her desk. At least as close to a scurry as someone Broni's size can get.

A few minutes later I had everything filled out and copied and assembled and was going out my office door when I was nearly flattened by Broni almost skidding to a stop in the doorway.

"Good grief, woman, you nearly mowed me down. What's your hurry?"

The words exploded breathlessly from her face. "I got it! I got it!"

"Calm down. What did you get?"

"The message! The message!"

Oh, boy. What do we do now. "From the bride Web site?"

"Ya! Ya!"

Apparently excitement either caused an echo or her brain had a loose wire.

"What did the message say?" I asked, hoping for just a single answer.

"It said they want me to submit a photo and they would be in touch."

"Let's go look at your message."

We went back to her office and read the message again.

"That's what it says, alright. Now, did you look at the pictures on the Web site?" I wanted to break it to her gently that we needed to find a good one.

"Ya, I did. They are all pretty."

"Exactly. Now doesn't it seem odd that there isn't an ugly one in the bunch? Are all the Latvian girls beautiful, with professional-looking photos?"

"I don't know. It doesn't seem quite right." Broni looked puzzled.

"Shouldn't some of these be from village girls with limited photographic resources at hand?"

"Maybe Mikelis makes them go to photographer before he posts the pictures?"

I thought for a moment, "I guess that's possible, but what if they are way out in the countryside somewhere and can't get to Mikelis and his photographer?"

"Yes, it is definitely a little strange."

It definitely is more than a little strange. I wandered back up to my office pondering this whole thing. It is obvious that Mr. Bosch knows more about this than he is letting on. Maybe it's time to talk to him again.

17 CHAPTER SEVENTEEN

I buzzed Broni's desk on the intercom, "Broni, can you come with me for a few minutes?"

"Why? Where are you going?"

"I want to talk to Mr. Bosch. At some point he may decide to let something slip about his fiancée."

"Oh, that's a good idea. I can leave for a short while."

"Ok, just tell Don you have to run to the drugstore or something so he doesn't ask questions."

"Ok."

I went outside and waited for her so our beloved manager wouldn't see us leave together. I didn't want to have to explain what we were doing.

After a minute Broni came out. We started walking the two blocks to Mr. Bosch's vacuum cleaner store. It was a lovely spring day. The blue sky and big white puffy clouds didn't fit in with our mission.

I opened the door to the Bosch Vacuum Cleaner Emporium and Broni followed me in. That is the real name of the business. I suspected Mr. Bosch took cocktail hour very seriously.

As the bell on the door rang, Mr. Bosch came out from the back room. "Hello, girls, what can I do for you?"

"Oh, Mr. Bosch, you just did it! You called us girls. We don't hear that too often anymore." I laid it on a little thick.

"Oh, Ophelia, you'll never age. You still look just like you did twenty years ago."

I wasn't flattered. I didn't look too good twenty years ago, either.

"Mr. Bosch, we came to talk to you because we are concerned. You haven't stopped in for coffee at the office in quite a while. It was the day that the dead guy was found in front of the building. Ever since, we haven't seen you. Also, you seemed worried about your fiancée arriving. In fact you said she would be here shortly and we've heard nothing about a wedding or even an engagement party."

Mr. Bosch looked decidedly panicky.

Broni spoke up, "We just want you to know we are worried about you."

He turned away from us and suddenly put his head down in his hands. We didn't quite know what to do.

"Mr. Bosch? What is it? Please tell us," I pleaded.

He looked up with a dreadful look on his face. "Come into my office."

He led us through the archway into the back room. Off to the side was a walled-off corner with a desk and a couple of chairs. This was his office. He sat down rather heavily in his desk chair and waved us into the other two old chairs. They both gave off ominously loud creaks when we sat down. Now I know why Emma Peel wears Spandex. It doesn't let the body bend very well, so it prevents a person's entire weight from resting on rickety chairs. Another factor may be that Emma Peel's body weight is about 40 percent of mine.

Mr. Bosch kept his head down and his eyes down while he began to speak. "I don't know how I let myself get into this. This is extremely embarrassing. I feel like a very old foolish man. It started about six months ago. Right here, on that computer there." He pointed to a laptop sitting on the side of his desk.

"I had just gotten a DSL line here at the store so I could send orders to my suppliers faster and get information for customers without waiting for e-mails to come from the companies. So, when the store was slow, I came back here and started surfing the Internet. I wondered what was so exciting that everybody was doing it."

He looked up at the blank wall before he spoke again. "My wife died two years ago. You might remember when it happened. She had been in a nursing home ever since she fell out the bus window on her way home from the vet's office. Her Pekingese took a flying leap while the bus was coming down East Avenue and she followed him."

We both shook our heads up and down. We remembered the incident very well.

"I have to admit I have been very lonely ever since. I've taken two or three ladies out to dinner, but the only ones I knew were my wife's friends and they are old, fat, and smelled like mothballs. One day I was looking around online and saw an ad for a dating service. One thing led to another and pretty soon I was hitting a lot of sites from other countries advertising women that were willing to come here and get married."

He turned to look at us and said, "This is extremely embarrassing, Oph. You must think I'm a complete idiot."

"Mr. Bosch, we can understand how lonely you were. Please don't be hard on yourself."

"Well, I got in deeper and deeper looking at pictures of beautiful young women. Before I gave it much thought, I was sending e-mail messages to a site advertising mail-order brides. They forwarded the messages to a girl, and she sent messages back. This went on for about a month and finally, like the old fool I am, I asked her to come here and marry me. It seemed like a good idea at the time. Then the people running the site asked me for the first payment. They said they needed money to start the process of getting her a passport and visa and also to cover their fees."

He turned back to stare at the desk again.

I asked, "How much money did they want?"

Mr. Bosch lowered his head and muttered. "The first payment was ten thousand dollars."

Broni and I looked at each other. I was thinking that there must be quite a lot of money in vacuum cleaners.

He continued, "I have made quite a lot of money in this store over the years. All the years Edna and I were married, we never took a vacation or had a new car. We lived in a small house over in your neighborhood, Broni. After she died, I felt guilty that she didn't get to enjoy what we had worked so hard for. In the early years, she worked here with me. When we took in vacuums on trade for a new one, she had to clean them out. I still remember her bent over the workbench over there with her little hands down in the dirt bags, digging for coins or lost jewelry. She did alright, too. She ended up with a couple of diamond rings and several dollars' worth of change over the years."

Good old Edna. Sounds like a great life.

"I decided that if I ever got married again, I would treat my second wife much better. So, I paid the ten thousand dollars and then bought a new house."

Broni spoke up, "Mr. Bosch, if you paid the money, then why has she not arrived?"

"After I paid them, I got more messages from Vija. That's her name, Vija."

"Beautiful," Broni said.

"Yes, it's a pretty name," I added.

"No, the name means 'beautiful' or 'fascinating,'" she corrected me.

"Please go on, Mr. Bosch," I urged.

"She said she was just graduating from college and needed

another couple of months to finish up. She had gotten a degree in some kind of biological science and had dreams of going on to medical school, but her parents died in a horrible reindeer accident so she couldn't go any further in school."

Reindeer accident? My little fraud-o-meter went off. I suspected those parents were alive and well and had no idea what kind of hustler they had raised.

He continued, "I told her that after we got married, she could go back to school right here at the university. It wouldn't be a problem. She said that made her very happy and she would see me soon. She even told me how much she had fallen in love with me just by reading my e-mails. Anyway, another month or so went by with more messages. I asked her when she would be arriving and she said it would be soon. In the last two months, she has put the date off twice. Now she says it will be about another three or four weeks. In the meantime, she has asked for money twice more."

"How much this time?" I asked

"It's always ten thousand dollars."

"Have you sent the last two payments?"

"Yes, Oph. I have, but about two weeks ago, I got a message asking for another ten thousand. This time she said she needed money for the plane ticket, to pay off her apartment lease and to buy all the clothes she would need. I objected a little. I told her she should be able to buy a plane ticket out of the thirty thousand I had already sent and she should wait until she got here to buy clothes, so she wouldn't have to pack them all."

At that point the bell on the front door rang. A customer was coming in. Mr. Bosch got up and went out to the front counter.

"Broni, what does this sound like to you?" I whispered.

"It sounds like she is just taking money and maybe never coming here or just using Mr. Bosch to be able to go to medical college here. I don't know which one."

"Whatever it is, it's about as crooked as you can get. "

Just then Mr. Bosch came back and addressed both of us. "Can you see why I didn't want to tell anyone? Old fools are the biggest fools."

"Why did you decide to tell us now?" I asked him.

"Because things are getting complicated. After I refused to send the most recent payment, she wrote back and said that it might take longer to get here if she couldn't get the money. Then, about two days later, a guy from Latvia shows up to collect the money in person."

I said, "Do you know his name, by any chance?"

"I think he called himself Michael or something that sounded like that. I guess it was a Latvian name. I didn't pay much attention."

"Did you give him the money?" I asked, even though I thought I already knew the answer.

"No. He came to my house, but I chased him out. I kind of lost my temper and swung a three-iron at him. Afterward, I realized I shouldn't have done that. I can't hit anything with a three iron. Also he's a lot younger and might have decided to fight back. Plus the fact that when I chased him out of the house I heard a lot of commotion in the wooded patch behind my house. He may have had some accomplices waiting back there. Anyway, I was so mad at him that I didn't stop to think."

Broni stared very intently at the floor when he mentioned the commotion in the woods.

"Well," I interjected, "I guess you're lucky the accomplices didn't come to his rescue. Have you seen him since?"

"No. He hasn't come back. Ophelia, I am afraid to go to the police. I don't know if what I did was illegal or not. Beside, I am so humiliated at being taken for a fool. I've spent thirty thousand dollars and have nothing to show for it."

"Have you heard from the girl lately?"

"No, not since the last request for money, before the guy showed up. I wonder if she ever intended to come."

"That's a good question. There's one other question, too. The day I tripped over the dead guy outside my office door, you stopped in for coffee, but ran out the door when we started describing the dead guy. Why did you take off like that?"

"I'm not sure. In fact, I'm not positive it's the same guy. Just about a week before you found him outside your office, I started seeing a man that sounded like your description kind of hanging around."

"What do you mean hanging around?"

"I first saw him when I opened up the shop one morning. He was standing outside the store next door. In a small town, you notice strangers. I didn't remember seeing him around before that. He walked past my store at least once a day and sometimes I would see him when I went down the street for lunch. I didn't see him anymore after the day you found him. Or at least I assume that was him."

"We do know who he was. Detective Crowley told us he was a representative of the Latvian government and was investigating something, but he wouldn't tell us what. Since then we have found out it has something to do with the guy you tried to whack with your three-iron His name is Mikelis, by the way. We know that also. And we know he used to live here, but went back home a while ago."

I didn't want to mention the part about Mikelis going home to make money. I think we just found out how he makes money.

"Ophelia, what am I going to do? If the man was investigating, they must know about me. Am I going to get arrested for concealing something? Is buying a bride illegal?"

"Mr. Bosch, I think the first thing you should do is go to the police. They already know some of this, but you could fill in a lot of the missing information. Broni and I have been doing a little research on this also. I don't think what you did was illegal. Rather unwise, maybe, but not illegal. In fact, Broni signed herself up to be a mail-order bride. We have to submit a picture for them to use on the Web site."

"You girls had better be careful. If they got that much money out of me, just think what is at stake for them," Mr. Bosch added.

Broni said, "I wondered how Mikelis could afford to fly here. It is expensive. Now I know that there is plenty of money for him to come here. Did you ever see anyone else with him?"

"No, I only saw him that once, when he came to my house. Why? Were there accomplices? I know I heard noises in back of my house."

"We think he did come here with another man, but I have a feeling he was traveling alone the night he came to your house. I wouldn't worry about those noises." I stood up. "Mr. Bosch, I know how hard this must have been for you to tell us all this. You don't need to be embarrassed. I'm sure the police have heard similar stories before."

He got up and stood in the doorway. "I will look just like one more old fool trying to get a young girl. They probably hear it all the time, but that doesn't make it any less embarrassing for me."

"Do you want us to go with you?" I volunteered.

"You don't think this is illegal?" he asked.

I thought back to our research on the Internet, "No, I don't think so. As long as you were just sending her money for expenses. Do you have a lawyer?"

"I thought I was just sending her money for expenses. Yes, I have a lawyer. Do you think I should call him first?"

"It wouldn't hurt to check with him before we go."

"Oph, would you go with me?" pleaded Mr. Bosch.

Broni looked a little insulted at being left out, but said, "Why don't you go right now? I have to get back to the office before I am missed."

"That's a good idea. Mr. Bosch, let's walk back to the office and I'll get my car." I didn't want to give him a chance to change his mind.

Mr. Bosch put the "Back in One Hour" sign on his front door, called his lawyer's office only to have to leave a voice mail, locked up the shop and off we went. No one spoke on the way back. I felt badly for him. This has to be humiliating for a local businessman to get caught up in looking at young women on the Internet. It was probably going on all over town, but not in public. Maybe he would be spared any newspaper coverage. Our town newspaper primarily reported on the attendance at Tupperware parties.

I unlocked my car for Mr. Bosch. I followed Broni into the office. I needed to get my purse.

Broni stopped in the middle of the lobby and said, in a voice for all to hear, "Now, Oph, don't you go holding hands with that detective again."

"Thanks a lot," I hissed. "Why don't you just tell the entire Western Hemisphere that we are involved in police stuff? And secondly, if I choose to hold hands, that's my business."

I turned and walked out the front door just as heads started popping out of office doors.

18 CHAPTER EIGHTEEN

I started up the car. Mr. Bosch sat silently staring out the window.

"Mr. Bosch, you know that these people are crooks. You shouldn't feel bad about what you did."

"Oph, you hear lots of stories about people trying to find love or companionship or whatever on the Internet. It always turns out with somebody getting taken. For me to fall into such a stupid trap just makes me feel like a real idiot. I just want to go get this over with and go home."

I couldn't argue with that. I guess Mr. Bosch couldn't either. At that moment, he yanked off his seat belt and flung open the car door.

"Oph, I can't do it. I need time to think and besides, I need to get a hold of my lawyer."

With that, he stepped out of the car and headed back to his store. I put my head down on the steering wheel. I felt so bad for him and his potential public humiliation. I tried to help him, plus I lost an opportunity to charm Detective Crowley. I figured I may as well go back into the office.

I walked through the front door and down the hall.

Broni swiveled her chair around when she saw me coming.

"What happened? Where's Mr. Bosch?"

I sat down in the old rickety chair against the wall.

"He flew the coop. He chickened out. Said he needed more time to think and wanted to talk to his lawyer."

"Oh. Too bad. I thought he was going to go."

"Me, too. I guess we just have to wait for him to be ready. I think we pushed as much as can for one day. Let's get a picture for you to send to the Web site. And let's not use any famous people this time."

"Yes. You had better pick it out. "

"Do you have any pictures of yourself when you were younger?"

"Yes, but just because I was younger doesn't mean they look like the girls on the Web site."

"How bad were they?" I think I could have phrased that better.

Broni huffed, "They weren't that bad. They just don't look like professional models."

"Ok, let's just get something off the Internet to use. There must be an obscure face somewhere."

I sat down at the computer on the other desk. After a few minutes I found a relatively wholesome-looking, only partially slutty blonde.

"Here's one. I'll send it to your machine."

"What? How can you do that?" Computers were not her strong point.

"Never mind. Just look in 'My Documents.' Look for the file name 'BroniPhoto.'"

She bent over her machine and started furiously clicking. "Here it is."

"Good. Now we need to change the file name to whatever you told them your name was."

"Ok, how do I do that?"

"Just give me the name and I'll change it."

We got the file name changed and the photo e-mailed off to the address on Mikelis' Web site. Now we wait.

"Broni. I'm going home. I think I'll just work outside for a while. I need to find some bushes I can glue to the garage door."

I packed up my briefcase and went home. Enough is enough. After hearing Mr. Bosch's story I was sure we could nail Mikelis and his merry band. Mr. Bosch's bailing out was a severe setback to our plans of crime-busting the mail-order bride ring.

Tomorrow is another day. Didn't somebody say that once? Fiddle-de-dee. I'll worry about this tomorrow.

Maybe tomorrow will bring an answer from the Web site. It will be interesting to see what they say. I dreamed about slutty-looking blondes chasing Mr. Bosch down the street while he threw big wads of cash back at them. I shouldn't drink herbal tea and eat chocolate just before going to bed.

19 CHAPTER NINETEEN

Morning came. I yawned and tried to go back to sleep. George and Ira hopped up on the bed simultaneously, causing a total of forty pounds of cat to land on my right knee. That pretty well ruled out going back to sleep. It nearly ruled out walking. As I got out of bed my knee did function, so I guess the damage was minimal.

I wanted to get to the office early to see if Broni had gotten any response from her picture. I bathed and decided to utilize all of my beauty secrets in case I had to come in contact with the detective today. Better safe than sorry. I took care to put on some of my more stylish clothing. Stylish is a relative term.

After all of us had eaten our breakfast, I gathered my stuff and set out for the office.

"Broni," I yelled from the front door. She came running down the hallway.

"What is it? What is wrong?" She screeched to a halt in front of me.

"Nothing. I just wanted to wake you up."

For my witticism I got a severe scowl. She started marching back to her office. I followed.

"Have you checked your e-mail yet today?"

She plopped down in her chair and started typing. "Not yet."

"Oh, I just wondered if you got any response from Mikelis."

"I am checking. Hang on to your ponies."

After a moment's thought I deciphered that one. "Did you mean hold your horses?"

"Whatever it is. You just hold anything you want. Maybe you'd rather hold on to that detective's hand?" She turned with a big strange smile on her face that kind of made her look like that woman who shoved Hansel and Gretel into the oven.

"Just check your e-mail."

She typed away for a minute and finally got her e-mail account open.

"No, there is nothing here from the address on the Web site. Maybe he is not answering messages until he gets home."

"Maybe. It's possible that he hasn't had a chance to check it," I said.

I sat down in the chair against the wall. Where do we go from here? I want to get Mr. Bosch to go to the police. Even if the bride thing isn't illegal, chasing down an old man and threatening him must be.

Just then the buzzer on the front door sounded. Someone was coming in.

"I'll go see who it is." I wandered up the hallway. It was Mr. Bosch.

"Hello, Oph. I wanted to apologize for running out on you yesterday."

"Mr. Bosch, that's understandable. It's not an easy thing."

"No, but that's no excuse. I just panicked, I guess. I do need to tell the police what I know. I thought about it all last night."

"That is certainly a noble attitude, and the right decision. Shall we go right now?"

"Perhaps we should. It will be good to get it done."

That is true. Plus I wanted the challenge of throwing some charm at Detective Crowley.

"I'll just go tell Broni I'm leaving."

I scurried back to her office and whispered, "Pssst, Mr. Bosch is here and wants to go the police, so I'm taking him. I'll be back."

She raised her eyebrows. "Off to see the detective, are we? Make sure you keep your mind on the case," she chuckled out loud at that one.

"Very funny. I'll talk to you later. I have to get him there before he chickens out again."

I trotted back to the front lobby.

"Were you able to talk to your lawyer?" I asked.

"Yes, he said to call him when we were leaving and he would meet us there. He said not to worry, it didn't sound serious."

"Ok, are we ready to go?"

Mr. Bosch nodded and we started out the door. Why hadn't I looked out the window before we came out? Just as we reached my car, I looked up and saw two men approaching us. One of them was Mikelis. They walked up to Mr. Bosch.

"We need to talk to you. We were just on our way to your shop," Mikelis said.

Mr. Bosch turned a little green around the gills. I was beginning to feel that way, too. This is just too close to bad guys for my taste. The man with Mikelis was a big one. Probably about six foot two or three and rather broad and disturbingly muscular.

"I can't talk to you right now. We are going somewhere."

I threw in my two cents, "Yes, we are late for an appointment."

They both looked in my direction and not in a very friendly manner.

The big one spoke with a thick accent, "You are going nowhere, old man."

That was right out of a B movie, I thought, but didn't bring that up. Another disturbing characteristic of this guy was the way he kept his hand in his jacket pocket with what looked like a finger pointing forward. It did occur to me that it was not his finger, but very possibly a firearm pointed at Mr. Bosch.

"We will all get in the car. You," he waved his pocket in my direction, "drive us to his store."

I gave thought, albeit briefly, to resisting the command. It just didn't seem like a good idea, so we all got in the car. Mikelis was in the front seat with me and the big guy was in the back with his coat pocket pressed against Mr. Bosch's side. I started the car and backed slowly out of the parking space. I wondered how long I could stretch out the two-block trip. I put the car in drive and started forward to pull out on to the street. Just then, a large black car pulled into the parking lot and parked in the space next to where my car had been. I looked quickly at the occupants. It was Alfred and Mother Fitch. I couldn't imagine what they were doing here. They didn't see me and I didn't dare roll down the window and call to them. I just kept going forward. As we pulled out onto the street, I saw Alfred helping his mother out of the car and handing her a cane.

I went as slowly as I could past the first corner, and down the street toward the Vacuum Cleaner Emporium.

The big guy growled from the back seat. "Go faster. Do not think of attracting attention to us, or this man could get hurt."

There must be a rash of old American gangster movies floating around the Baltic states. It sounded like this guy had seen several.

I turned the next corner and pulled into the alley behind the store. I turned off the engine and sat there. I was frantically thinking of what I could do to get us out of this fix. The big one growled from the back seat again. "Open the doors slowly and get out. Old man, unlock the door."

He hauled Mr. Bosch out of the backseat by his elbow, all the while keeping his jacket pocket up tight to his side. He pushed Mr. Bosch toward the back door of the store. Mr. Bosch was fumbling with his keys. Meanwhile I opened my door and got out. I didn't dare try anything in case that was a real gun.

Mikelis had been in the front seat with me. He got out and kept an eye on me while I walked around the front of the car. Mr. Bosch was unlocking the back door to his store. The big bad guy barked something at Mikelis in a decidedly foreign language. Mikelis moved around behind me and grabbed my elbow with what I considered excessive force. Mr. Bosch opened the door. His captor shoved him into the shop. Mikelis grunted and pushed my elbow forward.

"I'm moving," I protested.

"Go!" he barked back. Most unfriendly man I've run into in quite a while. I walked through the door into the back room where Broni and I had been just yesterday with Mr. Bosch spilling the beans.

The big one barked at Mikelis again and I felt myself being pushed over toward the workbench in the corner. He pushed Mr. Bosch in the same direction. Mikelis and the other guy, whose name we had not heard as yet - or if we had, it wouldn't register because not speaking their native tongue it would be difficult to pick out which guttural grunt might be a name - were jabbering at each other. It sounded as though the big guy was in favor of drastic action. Mikelis was shaking his head back and forth and yelled, "No, Oskar."

I hoped that meant he was vetoing something that could prove harmful to Mr. Bosch and myself. The big one, who we now know as Oskar, was clearly in charge and Mikelis' protests seemed to be getting weaker. Oskar shoved Mikelis toward our corner and pointed at a coil of rubber-coated electrical wire that was used to replace vacuum cleaner cords. I wondered if he was going to tie us up or just fry us on the spot. I was a little upset with myself for not coming up with an Emma Peel-like move to extract us from this predicament. Felling Mikelis with a swift kick like a Rockette on speed wouldn't help because the other guy had now taken his hand out of his pocket and there was a real gun in it. I looked at the contents of the workbench behind me. No tools were within my reach. The only thing I could reach was an old vacuum cleaner with its dirt bag sitting beside it, still full of dirt, fuzzy things, hair and stuff I didn't want to think about. I didn't think hitting Mikelis on the head with a soft cloth bag full of fuzz was going to help. Mikelis walked rather reluctantly to the roll of cord. It appeared that his heart was not really in this. Maybe I should let a few fetching tears spill down my cheeks to hasten the onset of his burgeoning sympathy. The problem is I am not that good an actress. I can't summon up tears on a moment's notice. My other thought was that in a few minutes I might not have to worry about my acting ability. The tears might be real.

"What do you want with us?" I heard myself asking.

"Shut up, woman," said the muscular, yet rude man named Oskar.

Mikelis picked up the roll of wire and began to pull several feet of it off. Just then, the bell on the front door sounded.

"Robert, are you here?" a voice I recognized as belonging to Alfred Fitch called out. Mr. Bosch looked at his captor. The big one whispered, "Go out there and be very careful what you say. Get rid of them or she gets hurt." That was said as the gun swung in my direction.

I could hear Mr. Fitch's footsteps as he walked toward the counter, but there was another noise I couldn't identify. Kind of a shuffle klunk, shuffle klunk. The only thing I could think of was Mother. She had a three-legged cane when I saw them in the parking lot a few minutes ago. This is no place for an old lady. I mean a really old lady, not just one my age.

Mr. Bosch walked out through the archway into the front of the store. We could hear him talking.

"Hello, Alfred. How are you? What can I do for you today? Out of bags again?" Mr. Bosch nervously rattled off.

"Just stopped in to say hello. I haven't seen you at the club recently. Do you think you'll have time for eighteen holes soon?" Mr. Fitch spoke in a very measured voice, not seeming to react to Mr. Bosch's agitation.

"I don't know. I've been busy lately fixing up my new house."

"While I'm here, did you ever get that old vacuum fixed up? Mother promised the cleaning lady we'd get it back soon. She likes it better than the new one I bought for her."

"Yes, I did. It's in the back. Why don't I bring it over on my way home this afternoon? It's kind of heavy."

"No, I'd rather take it now. I think the cleaning lady is coming later today."

"Uh, let me go back and make sure it's all put together. I may need to bring it later."

"Alright," Alfred said. As Mr. Bosch started back through the archway, Oskar, on one side and Mikelis on the other were watching him come through the curtain very carefully. The big guy grabbed Mr. Bosch's arm and pulled him to one side, out of the line of sight from the front room. Much to my surprise, and I would assume his also, a fist containing a gun appeared through the archway and smacked the big guy in the back of the head. His gun flew across the room. Mikelis started toward him. With a lightning fast burst of efficiency, I grabbed the dirt bag off the workbench and flung it into his eyes, severely limiting his ability to see the three-pronged cane that popped through the drape, snagged his leg and caused him to land hard on the concrete. As he hit the floor I heard a familiar cackle. The three-pronged cane appeared through the drape and landed on Mikelis' back. One of the prongs was sporting a rather sharp point instead of the matronly rubber tip of the other two. That particular one was positioned right on the back of Mikelis' neck and considerable force was being applied to it by Mother Fitch.

Mikelis started to squirm just a little and Mrs. Fitch pushed a harder. "I wouldn't wiggle quite so much, Sonny. I may be old but that thing is about half an inch away from cutting into something important."

The squirming stopped immediately. Meanwhile across the archway, Alfred Fitch was standing over Oskar with a gun pointed at his head.

"Thanks, Mother."

"Don't mention it, Alfred. What are mothers for?"

I finally summoned enough presence of mind to grab the roll of vacuum cleaner cord and wrap several lengths around Mikelis' ankles, then ran it around both wrists after he complied with Mother Fitch's wishes to put both hands behind him. I tied it as best I could and cut it with some pliers off the workbench.

"Miss Olsen, could I trouble you to wrap some of that around this gentleman's legs and arms as well?" Alfred asked.

"Of course, Mr. Fitch, it would be my pleasure." Oskar said something in his native language that I don't think should be translated in polite company.

The front door bell rang again. Mr. Bosch said, "I wish the door were that busy when I'm open for business." He peeked through the curtain and yelled, "Back here."

Detective Crowley, gun drawn, came flying through the drape and stopped short. I was bent over the big guy wrapping his wrists with enough electrical cord to power a small building and Mother Fitch was looking very pleased with herself while she kept the pointy prong firmly against Mikelis' neck.

"Fitch, I see you got here in time."

"Yes, Bert. These gentlemen were about to restrain Robert and Miss Olsen and perhaps do them some harm."

"Good afternoon, Bert," said Mother Fitch.

"Good afternoon to you, Mrs. Fitch. How have you been?"

"Fine, thank you, but I'm even better now. I haven't been in on a bust in quite a while. Can you cart these hooligans off to the pokey?"

"Yes, ma'am, I shall be happy to." He gestured to the uniformed men right behind him. They put handcuffs on Mikelis and his buddy and tried unsuccessfully to stand them up. I guess I had gotten a little carried away with the cord around the ankles. The policemen had to remove it before they could haul the evildoers out the door into the waiting squad car.

Alfred put his gun back in his pocket and Mother Fitch let out another little cackle. I walked over to the nearest chair and sat down. Embarrassingly enough, my legs were a little wobbly from the close call, but Mrs. Fitch was going strong.

Detective Crowley came over to me. "Ms. Olsen, are you all right?"

My first instinct was to tell him that I was so shaken, I would need him to put his two strong arms around me to calm me down.

"Yes, I'll be ok. It's just a little more excitement than I can handle in the afternoon."

I also was completely taken aback by our rescuers. Who knew that the Fitches were a crime-fighting team?

"Bert, I think you have things under control now. Robert, are you alright?"

"Yes, Al, I'll be fine, but I would like to know what's going on. What did those guys want with me? Was it just the money?"

"Robert, what do you say you come over for dinner this evening and I'll explain the whole thing. Mother hired a new cook, who seems to be able to turn out decent meals."

"That sounds like a good idea to me."

Detective Crowley spoke up. "Mr. Bosch, we'll need you to come to the station and explain exactly what has been going on from your perspective."

"Yes, of course," he said sheepishly. "I should have been there sooner. Ophelia tried to get me there yesterday but I didn't realize I would be putting both of us in danger. Oph, can you forgive me?"

I nodded. That was all I could muster up. I still had no idea what just happened. One minute we were in danger, the next we were being rescued by a hundred-year-old woman. I guess I'd better rethink my opinion of old ladies. I also needed to rethink my ability to stop evil in its tracks in the manner of Emma Peel. I had just witnessed a woman who had somewhere between twenty and forty years on me act a whole lot more like Emma Peel than I ever had.

"Ophelia, I will need a statement from you also," Bert said, still standing beside me.

I looked up at him. Where's the white horse? Isn't Bert supposed to come rescue me on a white horse?

"Ok." I was glad to find out I could still speak.

"Can you come to the station now? Perhaps you could bring Mr. Bosch and we could get both statements this afternoon," Bert asked.

"I can do that. My car is right out back."

Just then the front door bell went off. We all turned toward the curtain, not knowing what to expect next. The curtains flew apart and Broni came sailing into the room.

"Oph! Mr. Bosch! Are you alright? I told these people what I saw and he called the police and they told me to stay there and I could not stay there any longer ..."

"Broni, slow down. I'm confused enough," I said.

Alfred Fitch spoke up. "What Miss Zakresevskis is trying to say is that Mother and I came to your office to see you. When we went in, she was watching out the front window as you were forced into your car and drove off. She was rather excited and worried. After she told us the identity of the man she knew, Mikelis, Mother and I knew we had to get here right away. I called Detective Crowley from the car. I presume you did not expect to see two of your elderly clients in this capacity."

"No, I sure didn't. What is your capacity? Are you secret agents or something?"

Alfred laughed and Mother cackled. She had found a chair and was perching on it.

"That's a good one, Olsen. I like that. I always wanted to be a secret agent."

Alfred spoke again. "For many years, until my retirement, I worked for the CIA in several different capacities, both here and abroad. Since then, I have been occasionally called upon to help out with some cases. So I still do a little traveling because usually, they are not so close to home."

I had to find out how Mother Fitch got into this. "Mrs. Fitch, were you with the CIA also?"

The cackle again. "In a sense. Over the years I've helped Alfred with some cases. Whenever they needed an unlikely looking decoy, I filled in. I've done everything from carrying little cameras installed in my purse to film slave traders in Nairobi to wandering around downtown Moscow in a flowered hat looking like a lost tourist."

"Where did you learn to trip up criminals with your cane?"

"All old ladies know how to do that." She cackled again. "But also, before I could work for them I had to go through quite a lot of training in self-defense and how to use all kinds of weapons. I'm a dangerous old lady, Olsen."

I finally had to laugh. I couldn't believe Mrs. Fitch had been a real-life Emma Peel.

Bert was still standing beside me. He said, "Ophelia are you feeling well enough to drive now? I'd like to get those statements this afternoon."

"I'm fine. Just trying to sort out what happened and why. Are you going to be able to give me some answers?"

Mr. Fitch spoke, "Bert, why don't you and Miss Olsen come to our house this evening also. You can fill us in from your end and I will have talked to my people and we'll all have some answers."

Bert looked at me, "Would that be alright with you?"

"Yes, I'd like that."

Broni still stood in the archway. "Hrrmmph."

"Miss Zakresevskis, would you care to join us? I'm sure you also have questions."

"Yes, Mr. Fitch, thank you. I would like that."

"Ophelia, why don't I drive you and Mr. Bosch to the station? I think you both may be a little shaken up." Bert said. "I'll bring you back to get your car when we're done."

"Maybe that's a good idea. Come, Mr. Bosch, let's get this over with."

We three trooped out to the detective's car while the Fitches got into theirs and Broni walked back to the office. We all said goodbye and that we would see each other later.

At the police station, Bert questioned Mr. Bosch first. Apparently he got the whole story because it took them about half an hour. Then he came out and got me.

"Oph, I'll wait here in the lobby for you," said Mr. Bosch.

"Ok. I shouldn't be long."

Bert led me into his office and shut the door.

"Ophelia, you do know what a close call you had today?"

"I do now."

"Good. Tonight we'll try to put all the pieces together, but now I want you to tell me everything you have done or found out since I talked to you last."

"Well, I guess the major development would be that Mr. Bosch told Broni and me the whole story yesterday. That's when I tried to get him to come here, but he was mortified at being caught ogling young ladies on the Internet, so he ran out on me. So today things were going a little better and we were actually on our way here when Mikelis and the big guy named Oskar forced us into my car and made me drive to the vacuum cleaner store. That's about all I know."

"What exactly did Mr. Bosch tell you yesterday?"

"Just that he was lonesome and got started looking at Web

sites with pictures of young women. At some point he ran across the site that promised him a bride. So he ordered one, or whatever you do, then the demands for money started coming. The last time the girl wanted money, he told her to wait until she got here. That's when Mikelis showed up and demanded the money in person. Mr. Bosch said no and things went downhill from there. Now, what about the dead guy? That's what started this whole thing."

"You'll find out more tonight. Let's get both of you back to the store so you can pick up your cars. I'll have to come back and do paperwork and you need to relax. Go home and take a hot bath."

I was almost ready to ask if he'd like to join me, when my better instincts took over and I regained my civilized nature.

"That sounds like a good idea." Bert opened the door and I went out.

"Oph, can I pick you up tonight?"

As surprised as I was, there was a frisson of delight involved also.

"Yes, I'd like that. What time are we supposed to be there?"

"Alfred said about 6:30 for cocktails. I'll pick you up at 6:15. Is that alright?"

"That's fine. It's probably less than ten minutes to their house. Do you know where I live?"

"Yes."

Oh, really. I wonder how. Probably policemen have ways of finding things out. We walked out to the lobby.

"Ready to go?" Bert asked Mr. Bosch.

"Yes, I sure am."

We walked out into the sunshine, with me appreciating it even more than I had this morning.

20 CHAPTER TWENTY

Bert dropped Mr. Bosch and me off in the alley in back of the vacuum cleaner store.

"See you later," Bert yelled as he backed out of the alley and drove off.

"Do you want me to come in and help you clean up the dust I dumped?" I asked Mr. Bosch.

"No, Oph, I have lots of vacuum cleaners, remember?" He laughed.

"Oh, I guess that's right. I'll see you later then. I want to find out more about the Fitches' part in this."

"I've been friends with Al for a long time. I knew he used to do something like this, but I didn't realize he was still involved. So I want to hear more about this. See you later." He opened the back door and went in.

I got in my car and made my way back to the office. I was still a little shakier than I wanted to admit. I parked outside and went in to see Broni. She was sitting wide-eyed at her desk. When she saw me coming down the hallway she jumped up from her desk, ran up and gave me a big bear hug. I managed to extricate myself before my ribs gave way.

"Oph, I was so worried when I saw those guys get in your car with you. I was going to call the police but just then those clients of yours came in and I told them what I saw and they said they would take care of it."

"They did that, alright. I couldn't believe it when Mrs. Fitch nailed Mikelis and held him down." We both laughed. "I'm going home. It's nearly 4:30 and we're supposed to be at the Fitches' at 6:30."

"I will be there. I want to hear this whole story. Do you want me to pick you up? They live just down the street from Mr. Bosch, right?"

"Yes, we saw where they live that night we followed Mikelis. It's also my listing, so we have the address. And, no, Detective Crowley is picking me up." Here it comes.

"Oooooh, the detective is picking you up? Are you going to invite him in? If you don't show up for dinner, we will come looking for you."

"Alright, that's enough. No, I am not going to invite him in. He's just doing it because he thought I would maybe still be upset."

"Then why is he letting you drive home now?"

"Because. Just because." I turned to leave. "I'll see you later."

"Ooooh, ok. Do not be late." She gave an evil giggle.

"Bye."

I drove home feeling exhausted. I don't know how Emma Peel still looks as fresh after her adventures as before. Being in the presence of bad people takes a lot out of you.

I walked in the house and was greeted by a chorus of chirps. "Not suppertime yet."

They followed me up the stairs and sat on the bathroom floor as I turned on the water.

"You can sit here while I take a bath and then we'll get supper. I'm eating out tonight."

In my bedroom I shed my clothes and put on my robe. I went back to the bathroom and poured some spearmint and eucalyptus bath oil into the running water. The bottle said it will provide a relaxing aroma. I was skeptical but it's worth a try. I slid into the hot water and leaned back. It is an old tub with a sloped end. The hot water felt good. I think maybe that aroma is relaxing. I certainly felt much better. So good, in fact, that I dozed off for a few minutes and woke to protestations of the dinner postponement.

I lathered my whole body with body wash, also spearmint and eucalyptus. It certainly did smell good. After washing it all off, I reluctantly got out of the tub. I looked at my watch and was startled to find out it was quarter to six. I only had one half hour to get lovely, or find some new beauty secrets. I started plowing through my closet to find something that would render Bert absolutely helpless in the face of my stunning appearance. That didn't work out very well, so I settled for something that would be less than hideous.

I checked my watch again. It was about five after six. I went downstairs with the troops following and gave them their supper.

Promptly at 6:15, the doorbell rang. I opened the kitchen door, then descended with fluid grace to the back door. In one swooping move, I turned the knob and swung the door open so the lower corner caught my ankle right on that bone that sticks out. Apparently my face registered the pain I was feeling.

"Oph, are you alright? You can't let these guys get to you. They're locked up now. They can't hurt you." He stepped through the door and took my elbow.

I started to laugh as I pointed down at my ankle bone, which was already turning a peculiar shade of purple.

Bert looked down and gently swung the door shut. I felt good to get the corner out of my ankle. Much to his credit, he didn't actually laugh out loud. Instead he moved just a little bit closer. I looked up and found him staring at my eyes. I was wondering if there was something wrong with them. I probably had makeup smeared all over or something. I was ready to go up the steps into the kitchen and find a mirror, when Bert leaned down and kissed me. Not in a long, pressure-filled passionate way and not in a perfunctory pecking way, but in a nice, medium-long, feel-good way. Apparently my response, as unconscious and instinctual as it may have been, pleased him. He drew back and smiled. I smiled too, but self-consciously.

"Come in," I said as I walked up into the kitchen. "Meet my friends." George and Ira were just finishing their dinner.

"Well, hello there, cats. What are their names?"

"George and Ira. They're the Gershwin brothers."

Bert knelt down and petted George. Ira is a little more timid, but gradually approached Bert and both got petted. So, he likes cats.

Bert stood up. "Oph. I may have been a little bit forward, but did I observe correctly that you were not offended?"

I am completely out of practice at this kind of thing. I have been divorced for many years and pretty much avoided any complications of this sort in my life. For some reason, I didn't mind now having to summon up some charm, if possible, and no, I most certainly was not offended.

"No. You observed correctly. I was not offended."

"And would you be offended if it were to happen a second time?"

Here I am, turning into a brazen hussy right in my own kitchen.

"There's a good possibility that I would not be offended."

So, this time Bert stepped in pretty close, put his arms around me in a most theatrical manner and proceeded to plant a big one. How does one gracefully put a stop to something that you don't really want to put a stop to? If this were to continue, I was afraid we could be very late for dinner. So, I just relaxed and enjoyed myself. Alas, it too soon came to an end. Bert stood back with little gleam in his eye. Apparently he had been having a good time, too.

"Oph, as much as I would like to continue, I think we'd better go."

"I think you're right. This could get out of hand."

He stopped and looked at me with a slow smile creeping across his face. We went out the back door to Bert's car.

21 CHAPTER TWENTY-ONE

We chatted away on the trip to the Fitches' house. Bert pulled up in the driveway. Broni's car was at the curb in front of the house with another one I thought was Mr. Bosch's. We walked up to the front door and rang the bell. Bert still had a slight grin on his face.

Mr. Fitch answered the door. He looked very dapper in a dinner jacket and tie.

"Good evening. So glad you're here. Please come in."

We stepped over the solid oak threshold and into the foyer.

"Good evening, Alfred," Bert said.

"Good evening, Mr. Fitch." I figured I'd better be a little more formal, since he was my client.

"Please call me Alfred. All my friends do. Come into the library. We're having drinks in there tonight. Mother is regaling Bronislawa and Robert with tales of her derring-do."

This I want to hear. We followed Alfred across the foyer, through the living room and into the beautiful library. I could never get tired of seeing this room. Sitting on the long, low, leather sofa in front of the row of windows that looked out on the gardens was Broni. She had on her best dress. It was light green with big maroon cabbage roses all over it. In a matching club chair - it matched the sofa, not Broni's dress - was Mr. Bosch. Mother Fitch sat in a wing chair next to Mr. Bosch.

"Good evening, Mrs. Fitch, Mr. Bosch, Ms. Zakresevskis," Bert said as he made a half circle around the room.

"Mrs. Fitch, Mr. Bosch. Hi, Broni," I said.

"Hello, Oph. Not late, I see."

I gave her a look hoping to discourage any more comments. I walked over to the couch and sat down in the middle of it. Bert followed and sat on the end.

"What can I get you to drink, Detective?" Alfred asked.

"Would you have scotch?" Bert responded.

"Yes, of course. Would a 21-year-old single malt do?"

Bert's eyes widened. "That would do very nicely."

"Miss Olsen, what will you have?"

"Perhaps I'll have just a tiny touch of the same."

Bert's eyes widened even more. He looked at me. I smiled in my usual charming fashion.

Alfred brought our drinks and proposed a toast. "To all our continued good health."

We raised our glasses, including Mrs. Fitch, who appeared to have a good dose of the 21- year-old Scottish whisky.

Alfred situated himself in a comfortable-looking chair at one end of the group before he spoke. "We are waiting for one more guest. I have invited the gentleman who is the head of security at the Latvian Embassy in Washington. He was involved in this investigation due to the murder victim on your front sidewalk." He looked at Broni and me.

Just then the doorbell rang and Alfred went to answer it, returning a couple of minutes later with a tall, way-beyond-handsome gentleman.

"I would like to introduce Ojars Dreimanis. He has been involved in the investigation from the beginning." Alfred then introduced all of us to him. Bert already knew him.

"Good evening. Mr. Bosch, Miss Olsen, Miss Zakresevskis, Mrs. Fitch. How are you, Bert." He walked over and shook Bert's hand before taking a seat.

"Now that we are all here, I think we could begin filling everyone in on the details," Alfred said, his eyes scanning the room. "I know that Miss Olsen and Miss Zakresevskis have not been privy to all the information because of the ongoing investigation. I expect you have some questions."

"You're right about that. I have a lot of questions." I looked over at Broni for some support and found her staring googly eyed at Mr. Dreimanis. "And so do you, right, Broni?"

"Oh, yes, of course." She finally took her eyes off him.

I looked back at Alfred. "First of all, who was the dead guy on our front sidewalk?"

"Alfred, if I may?" Mr. Dreimanis said. "He was an agent of my government. He had been sent here to follow Mikelis and his cohort, Oskar, and find out what they were doing. Mr. Bosch, you may have seen him walking around in the village, paying particular attention to your store. The reason for that was we had accessed some of Mikelis' e-mail messages and the replies. So we knew some of his victims."

Mr. Bosch spoke up. "But the messages were from the girl. Was she using his account to send them out?"

Mr Dreimanis and Alfred looked at each other and nodded. Alfred spoke, "Robert, there was no young lady. The messages were all from Mikelis' account, using a girl's name. The pictures on the Web site were just models. Not actual mail-order brides. Also, Miss Zakresevskis, don't wait for a response from Mikelis. The application you filled out was just a decoy. I'm afraid your bid to become a mail-order bride fell on deaf ears."

Broni's face turned a vivid shade of fuchsia. Bert turned and looked at me. I shrugged my shoulders to proclaim my innocence.

"Mr. Fitch. My application was just a ploy to bring Mikelis and his scheme out into the open and perhaps trap him," Broni protested. "I really do not want to be a mail-order bride. Really I do not."

Mrs. Fitch cackled. "I bet you would if you had the chance. I wouldn't mind trying it."

Alfred just shook his head. Everyone else laughed. Except Broni.

Bert whispered in my ear, "Did she really sign up?

I nodded and whispered back. "We found a picture on the Internet and sent it in."

He closed his eyes and sighed.

Mr. Dreimanis finished his story. "Our agent was following Mikelis and Oskar. From what we could piece together from the reports he filed, he had been observing the neighborhood of Mr. Bosch's shop. He was also observing your office, Miss Zakreveskis, because he had something to return to you. He apparently was attacked and murdered while he was on his way to see you. From the story that Mikelis told this afternoon, Oskar climbed up the ladder on the back of your building and took a large piece of ice off the roof and dropped it down on the agent's head, while he was outside your office. Oskar had been following the agent that morning to determine his movements."

Bert spoke up. "I can fill in some of the details here. The day after the body was discovered in front of the real estate office, some of our investigators came back to the building to check out the theory that the ice was a possible murder weapon. Broni, do you remember a man telling you he was from a company that had been called by the landlord to repair the roof? "

"Yes, I do. I did not get suspicious because the landlord sends people once in a while to check the roof. We can hear them walking around up there. Was that your people?"

"They were. We wanted to keep it quiet. It's a good thing we did, because you two got yourselves involved enough as it was." Bert looked at me. "In any case, the investigative team found that the piece of ice in the parking lot had some small stones and tar stuck to it. That led us to believe it came off the roof, yet there was no visible ice hanging over and it had been too warm for icicles. They found an area on the roof that was shaded from the sun, next to the front parapet. There was ice remaining in that area which had the same stones and small pieces of tar that stuck to it when the technicians pulled it off the roof. At that point we were pretty sure we were looking at murder, because there was no way that ice could have fallen by itself."

Broni spoke, "You said this man was returning something to me? Did I know him?"

Mr. Dreimanis smiled at her. "I can answer that. No, you did not know him. What he was returning to you was the bracteat that Miss Olsen found by his body. It belongs to you."

"How could it belong to me?" she said.

"Many years ago, your grandmother had some of her collection of these old Livonian coins stolen. Do you remember anything about that?"

"Yes, a little. I was very young. I think some of my older cousins had stolen them to sell."

"That is correct. There were only five stolen. The local police in your grandmother's village were to return the coins to her when the trial was over. They could only find four. To cover up their sloppy handling of the evidence, they found a little foil covered chocolate coin that greatly resembles a bracteat. So they gave her four authentic coins and one candy."

"But that is impossible. Just last week Oph and I checked through all the coins to make sure they were there."

"Broni, we didn't actually take them out of the little boxes, remember, you said we'd get fingerprints on them or some such thing."

She looked thunderstruck.

"Believe me, Miss Zakresevskis, you are missing a coin. The small police department was disbanded recently and we found written evidence from the former police chief that they did commit this fraud so they would not be embarrassed. It was somewhat unusual that they kept records of the deception, but we were very grateful that they did. Even more fortunately, the bracteat was eventually located, but by then your family had immigrated to the United States. So it sat in an evidence box for many years."

Alfred chimed in. "Your coin was sent to the Latvian Embassy in Washington with instructions to return it to you. Through relatives in the village, it was determined that you now had your grandmother's collection and they also provided your address.

Lucky for you that you still correspond with them."

"So he was returning the coin to her. What connection does that have with Mikelis and Oskar?" I asked, still somewhat puzzled.

"Absolutely none," said Mr. Dreimanis. "It was just his bad luck to have his guard down that morning. He was standing there looking at your display in the window, probably, before he came into the office. That gave Oskar enough time to run up the ladder in the back and rip a piece of ice off the roof and throw it down on the poor man's head. After Mr. Bosch had refused to pay them any more money, Oskar was beginning to panic. He wanted to get this agent off the case. "

I still needed to know more. "So where did Mr. Bosch's money go? Directly to Mikelis and the other guy?"

"Precisely, Miss Olsen." Alfred was talking again. "It was simply fraud. They set up several e-mail accounts and used them over and over to make their victims think the messages were from the brides. But when Robert objected to sending any more money, they decided to make a trip over here and try to collect. If they had not gotten greedy, they may never have gotten caught."

"To say nothing of also being charged with murder," Bert said.

"Why was Mikelis running around by himself that night that Broni and I were observing him?" I asked no one in particular.

Bert answered. "Because Oskar was keeping a low profile after the murder. Which was very lucky for you, Mr. Bosch, because if Oskar had been along, you may not have gotten away with just chasing him out. It appears that Oskar is a far more ruthless character than Mikelis."

"I think the other guy may have been hiding outside, because there was a ruckus out in the little wooded patch behind my house," Mr. Bosch added.

Bert, Alfred and Mother Fitch started to laugh. Broni and I kept our heads down.

"What's so funny about that?" Mr. Bosch questioned.

"Robert, the noise in the woods was merely our intrepid sleuths, the Misses Olsen and Zakresevskis, trying to track Mikelis' movements," Mr. Fitch explained.

"Sorry, Mr. Bosch. But Bert asked us to report on anything unusual and we were just trying to help."

"Let the record show that I most certainly did not ask you to tail dangerous suspects all over the city. You were just supposed to keep your eyes open, particularly in the Latvian community." Bert was quite adamant about the distinction.

"Nice going, Olsen. I would have done the same thing," Mrs. Fitch piped up and we all got a laugh. Just then a bell rang in a box on the wall.

"Hey, Alfred, we finally got one that can figure out how to work the ringer," Mother Fitch said.

Alfred addressed us all. "What Mother means is that the new cook has figured out how to signal us that dinner is served. Let's all go enjoy what we hope will be a delightful meal."

"Don't hold your breath. The last one made everything taste like dog food," said Mother

I wondered if she used that can I saw in the refrigerator. I hope the new cook used something else.

We had a delightful and delicious dinner. Everyone was talking back and forth about how a rather simple case of fraud and greed turned into murder.

After dinner we retired to the library again to have an after-dinner drink.

Mr. Dreimanis was the first to say good night. "Alfred, thank you for a delightful evening. I will see you tomorrow to finish up any reports we may need. Bert, thank you for your diligent investigation, and it was a pleasure working with you. Miss Zakresevskis and Miss Olsen, I am very glad you came to no harm during this adventure. Perhaps next time you should heed the warnings of your detective. Mr. Bosch, I am glad we were able to apprehend these gentlemen before they did you any more harm. We are hoping to recover most of your money and return it to you. Good night, all."

As Alfred walked him to the front door, Mother Fitch laid into

Mr. Bosch. "Robert, I hope you learned a lesson from this. You need to go out and find a woman in person and make sure she's close your own age."

"Mrs. Fitch, believe me. No more surfing the Internet to find anybody."

Bert looked at me. "Shall we?"

It was all I could do to refrain from coming up with a totally inappropriate answer.

I stood up. "Mrs. Fitch, this has been a thoroughly delightful evening. Thank you."

"It was fun, Olsen. Now, when are you going to take me to see condos? The ones with the good-looking doormen?"

"I'll set up some appointments and call you tomorrow."

"And don't mind Alfred when he tells you our condos have to be side by side. He wants to keep an eye on me. I just might want to invite that doorman up for a little drink." She cackled mightily at that one.

"I'm sure you would, Mrs. Fitch. We'll go check out the doormen," I said as I laughed with her.

We started for the front door. Mrs. Fitch spryly got up from her chair and came along. Much to my surprise, she was not using her walker or a cane.

I was watching her walk when she noticed and said, "What's the matter, Olsen? My act with the walker was a slight exaggeration. I don't really need it around the house, but being involved in the investigation, I needed to promote the idea that I was pretty feeble. I do need the cane when I go out, particularly when I need to trip up somebody." She smiled.

Alfred opened the front door for us. "Good night, Miss Olsen, Miss Zakreveskis, Bert. Thank you for joining us this evening."

"Thank you for having us," I said as I stepped out the door. Bert stepped out and walked ahead of me.

Mrs. Fitch leaned out the door and grabbed my elbow. "Hang on to that one, Olsen."

I whispered back, "I'll try. Good night."

Broni was snickering by this time. Bert had stopped and waited for me.

"Broni, where are you parked?" Bert asked her.

"Oh, I am right here in front of the house." She pointed at the huge machine at the curb.

"Ah, I see. In fact how could I have missed it?" Bert laughed.

We started toward the driveway. "Good night, Broni," I called.

"Good night, Oph. Don't be late for your floor time tomorrow." Wiggling her eyebrows in what she thought was a sophisticated manner.

I looked at Bert to find him smiling. "Good night, Broni."

ABOUT THE AUTHOR

K. K. Wolfe is a real estate salesperson in New York State. She resides in a Victorian house constantly in need of repair. The other inhabitant is a cat.